A NOVEL BASED ON THE LIFE OF

GUGLIELMO MARCONI

MARCONI
AND HIS MUSES

Pamela Winfrey

The Mentoris Project
Barbera Foundation, Inc.
P.O. Box 1019
Temple City, CA 91780

More information at www.mentorisproject.org

ISBN: 978-1-947431-05-8

Library of Congress Control Number: 2017956760

The Mentoris Project is a series of novels and biographies about the lives of great men and women who have changed history through their contributions as scientists, inventors, explorers, thinkers, and creators. The Barbera Foundation sponsors this series in the hope that, like a mentor, each book will inspire the reader to discover how she or he can make a positive contribution to society.

Contents

Foreword

First and foremost, Mentor was a person. We tend to think of the word *mentor* as a noun (a mentor) or a verb (to mentor), but there is a very human dimension embedded in the term. Mentor appears in Homer's *Odyssey* as the old friend entrusted to care for Odysseus's household and his son Telemachus during the Trojan War. When years pass and Telemachus sets out to search for his missing father, the goddess Athena assumes the form of Mentor to accompany him. The human being welcomes a human form for counsel. From its very origins, becoming a mentor is a transcendent act; it carries with it something of the holy.

The Mentoris Project sets out on an Athena-like mission: We hope the books that form this series will be an inspiration to all those who are seekers, to those of the twenty-first century who are on their own odysseys, trying to find enduring principles that will guide them to a spiritual home. The stories that comprise the series are all deeply human. These books dramatize the lives of great men and women whose stories bridge the ancient and the modern, taking many forms, just as Athena did, but always holding up a light for those living today.

Whether in novel form or traditional biography, these books plumb the individual characters of our heroes' journeys. The power of storytelling has always been to envelop the reader in a vivid and continuous dream, and to forge a link with the subject. Our goal is for that link to guide the reader home with a new inspiration.

What is a mentor? A guide, a moral compass, an inspiration. A friend who points you toward true north. We hope that the Mentoris Project will become that friend, and it will help us all transcend our daily lives with something that can only be called holy.

—Robert J. Barbera, President, Barbera Foundation
—Ken LaZebnik, Founding Editor, The Mentoris Project

Prologue

JULY 20, 1937

As he lay dying, Guglielmo Marconi wished he had paid more attention to the mechanics of his own body. He wished he had listened to the obvious evidence that not all was well. He could have approached it like a mechanical problem. He could have tinkered and tested, using different chemicals, materials, techniques. He could have found a way out of this mess. Instead, he was lying in a cold bed with stiff white sheets that smelled of bleach. He knew a wooden cross hung on the wall above his bed, although he could not see it.

Someone down the hallway was clanking. The sound echoed, clattering and bouncing off the cold pale green walls. Bedpans, Marconi thought. Some young blond nurse is soiling her lovely hands with bedpans.

In his imagination, she was like a bird. Flitting around some lucky man's bed, twittering to him to lift his spirits. He thought he could hear a whispering song in an upper register, accompanying the sharp metal sounds. It was a kind of aria. He felt that only he could discern this fluttering song. Only he could hear the slight sound waves. He concentrated. They drifted over the footsteps that receded down the hallway. They floated above a conversation between two men who were speaking in low tones, one a baritone, one a bass. It was like a little opera. An opera sung only for him. He heard her trill one more short, papery note, and then she fell silent. The aria was over.

He sighed and became aware of his breath, his lungs like a farrier's bellows, the inhale a different cadence than the exhale. For sixty-three years, those bellows had done their work without fail. Their regularity and constancy were something to be amazed at. Machines were far more prone to breaking down and required constant supervision, yet this apparatus had been as regular as a clock.

So unlike his heart, which had let him down repeatedly. It came as no surprise. It was built badly from the start. A flaw in the wiring. First Annie, his mother, then Alfonso, his brother, and now he was suffering from a badly made "ticker," as the Americans called it. He became aware of his heart's rhythm. He sensed the irregularity, the abnormal quality of its beat. The pressure behind his breastbone was something he had grown used to—if one could grow used to feeling that an elephant was sitting solidly on his chest. He focused exclusively on his heart and heard the way it tripped slightly, like children trip and then catch themselves without missing a beat. And then he could not hear it. He threw his arm over his head, hoping his gesture would somehow increase his ability to hear.

He became aware of someone standing near him and opened his eyes to see Dr. Frugoni, cleaning his glasses on his white lab coat. Marconi said, "How is it, Frugoni, that my heart has stopped beating while I am still alive?"

Frugoni put his thick glasses back on and looked carefully at Marconi before answering. He cleared his throat and said,

"Don't ask such questions. It is only a matter of position, because your forearm is raised."

Marconi closed his eyes again. "No, my dear doctor, this would be correct for the veins but not for an artery," he said. "But I don't care. I don't care at all."

And the odd thing was, he didn't care. He didn't care about his heart. He didn't care about his lungs. All he cared about was the aria the beautiful nurse was singing, for she had begun again. This time, there was no accompaniment. This time, she sang a classic Italian aria. He thought it might be "L'amour est un oiseau rebelle" from *Carmen*. Love is a rebel bird, he thought. The song enveloped him.

He could picture the nurse as she sang. She went to the windows, threw them open, and let in a flock of birds, each one with more brilliant plumage than the last. They filled the hospital room with color. Vibrant teal, crimson, and a bright yellow that contrasted with the vermillion green of the hospital walls. They swirled into the room, lured by the golden song. Their wings made a carpet of notes. The nurse unpinned her nurse's cap and released her hair, which flowed around her face as though in a soft wind created by the birds. She looked Marconi squarely in the face and smiled.

Chapter One

THE BOY MIRRORS THE MAN: 1879

They say the boy mirrors the man, and as the boy dug in his heels, the saying was true. Guglielmo Marconi, five years old, was playing tug-of-war with his dog, Bella. She was a bulldog, as stubborn as he was, and they had been pulling on a red cotton cloth for over fifteen minutes. Thin, wiry, with arms like sticks of wood, the boy held on, refusing to give up.

They were on the sprawling lawn of Villa Griffone, the Marconi home outside of Pontecchio Marconi in Tuscany. The boy's mother, Annie, sat at a table nearby, sipping tea and watching with amusement. The boy was just like Bella. Nothing would make him veer from something he wanted. She poured another cup, added a lump of sugar from the rose petal sugar bowl, and called out, "Guglielmo, perhaps you and Bella should call this one a tie. You are wearing her out!"

Guglielmo shook his head and tugged even harder. But Bella had had enough. She abruptly let go, and Guglielmo fell backward and rolled into a rosebush. Annie rushed over. After making sure he was all right, she fed him a slice of *Schiacciata alla Fiorentina*, a sponge cake that smelled of orange peel and vanilla. He forgot all about the rosebush scratches and climbed into his mother's lap. She smelled of rosewater and lilacs. He buried his face in her neck. Here was a place of safety.

At the dinner table, he always sat at her right, and she always gave him the best part of the braciole. She made sure he had enough raisins and pine nuts to spread on the thin layers of beef, and she added a thick layer of butter to his bread.

His father, Giuseppe, a glowering presence at the other end of the table, gave rolling accounts of the livestock, the vineyards, and the fig trees. He complained about the tottering gardener, the inebriated stableboy, and the way the scullery maid looked at the inebriated stableboy. He complained about the fall of grape prices, the rust infestation on the fig trees, the way that the dust from the road gave him a headache. Guglielmo tried to stay far away from him, but at dinner, everyone was expected to attend.

His brother, Alfonso, always sat at the right of their father. Nine years older than Guglielmo, Alfonso was positioned where he could see Guglielmo clearly. Sometimes Alfonso raised his eyebrows. This was a sign that Guglielmo should stop whatever he was doing—kicking the table legs, squirming, tapping his knuckles on the tabletop—that would draw his father's unwanted attention. When Alfonso's eyebrows became a flock of crows rising suddenly from the field, something was seriously wrong.

Alfonso had taught Guglielmo how to rub his fingers along the rim of a crystal wine glass and make it sing. If he rubbed with just enough pressure, he could feel the vibrations, the voice of the glass. After that, Guglielmo could not stop finding wine glasses and rubbing them. With the help of his mother, he lined up all the wine glasses in the house on the family sideboard. He discovered that if he filled the glasses with varying levels of liquid, they would sing different pitches. He and Annie managed to play the first few notes of *Il Barbiere di Seviglia*, which was so funny to young Guglielmo he fell laughing to the floor.

Once, Guglielmo made the mistake of trying to replicate the fun with his mother's wine glass at the dinner table. He was so focused on the glass that he missed the frantic wiggling of Alfonso's eyebrows. His father roared his displeasure and sent Guglielmo from the table without supper. Later that night, his mother brought him an illicit bowl of ziti. She sat on the side of his bed and explained while his father was a good man, he was also a stern man who did not understand the wrigglings of a young boy. He had been an old soul from birth, she said. One who treasured quiet, order, and a solemn, decorous demeanor at all times. It would not do to cause ripples. She left him with those thoughts after kissing him on the forehead.

Guglielmo flopped back in his bed and stared at the ceiling. Why couldn't life be more like the singing of the wine glass? A mysterious sound coaxed from an unlikely source. Who would have even known it was there? It had always been there at the dinner table. All those years, it had sat there, undiscovered, hidden within the thin walls of curving crystal. All those dinners with multiple unsung voices waiting to be activated, waiting to be played.

There were sights that no one could see. Sounds that no one could hear. There were mysteries and deep, dark caves to explore. There were thoughts that no one had ever thought before. The world was filled with the unknown, the yet to be discovered. His heart was on fire and his body seemed to heat up, fueled by these ideas. His mother understood. She would shield him from his father. She would make it possible for him to find the next song.

Chapter Two

FLYING HIGH: 1881

The kite was a thing of beauty. Guglielmo and his mother had spent the day crafting it. He had enjoyed the geometry. Folding the paper so it made a square, measuring the dowels, tying them into a 90-degree angle, positioning the cross, which his mother said was like the cross of Christ, cutting the paper into a diamond, taping the dowels into place—all of it had a satisfying cadence. He loved the combination of doing something with his hands and challenging his brain. It was just a kite, but there was something amazing about its ability to fly, to use a simple physical structure to command the wind.

At the age of seven, Guglielmo was constantly asking questions. As he worked on the kite, his analytical mind actively considered issues of torque, mass, velocity, speed, and tensile strength. He was like one of those Christian Crusaders his mother had told him about, always on a quest. He was driven to learn, hungry for facts, always imagining how to put them to use.

The next morning, Annie stood on a hill, holding the kite high. A storm had passed in the night, refreshing and invigorating the air. It was a perfect day to fly a kite. Guglielmo took the end of the string, turned, and ran, his short legs pumping so hard he slipped out of one shoe. The kite, a simple, utilitarian white, flew from Annie's hand and stood out against the sapphire sky. She walked toward him, her red hair catching the light, her long skirts darkening from the dew. She was his protector, his companion, his savior. Ignoring the damp, she sat down in the long grass, shielded her eyes from the sun, and gazed up at the kite.

Guglielmo began to experiment, pulling the kite string so the kite dipped and danced. Annie started to laugh. Her laugh was as musical as her singing voice. It was the kind of laugh that made other people laugh as well. Guglielmo began to laugh in response, and the two could be heard all the way down to the shed where Piero, the blacksmith was working on the ancient plow. Piero looked up, hammer in hand, and smiled. On a morning like this, it was good to be alive.

Chapter Three

THE DINNER PLATE EXPERIMENT: 1882

The kitchen in the Marconi home was guarded over by Maria, the cook. Contrary to most great cooks, Maria was thin. Rumor had it that she poured all her calories into the one thing she owned of value, a solid gold filigreed cross that hung below the hollow of her neck. If she had been a jackdaw, the kitchen would have been her nest, for she guarded it with a zealous and possessive eye.

Guglielmo rested his cheek against the stuccoed wall in the hallway outside the kitchen and listened. He could hear Maria's heels as she walked back and forth between the stove and the butcher-block table. It was still before dawn, and she had beaten him to the punch. How was he going to get the plates? This was no small task. The family plates resided in a cupboard off the kitchen, and the kitchen was rarely unoccupied. Activities began before sunrise as Maria began making bread for the day and various laundresses, scullery maids, stableboys, groundskeepers, butlers, and bootboys sailed through the place as though it was a busy harbor.

At 2:00 a.m., Guglielmo sprang from bed like a jack-in-the-box. The cold stone floor under his feet sent an additional jolt through him. Using the light of the moon, he stole softly down the stairs.

He stopped at the corner just before the kitchen and listened. He heard the *kyok-kyok-kyok* of a nightjar and the sawing of cypress branches as they chafed in the wind, but the kitchen was quiet. As silent as an owl on the hunt, he sprinted to the kitchen cupboard. Opening it quickly, he was startled when one of the hinges squeaked. He froze and caught his breath. But there were no sounds from upstairs, only the velvety stillness of a full-moon night. As he gathered up ten plates, he wondered at their weight. The family crests on the rim turned into disapproving eyes. He covered the plates with a dishcloth and, balancing them with difficulty, took them outdoors.

A warm breeze came from the direction of Bologna. The moon shone like a 5,000-lira coin, and he could see easily.

Even at a young age, Guglielmo was a planner, and he had sketched out exactly what was to happen next. Down the road and over the first rise sat an old springhouse. Made of hand-hewn stone, it was seldom used and was the perfect place to hide the materials for his next experiment. The plates were heavy, something he had not calculated on, and he had to rest several times before he made it to the springhouse door. Once inside, he laid them carefully on the dirt floor next to the rest of his equipment. Coils of wire, wire snips, and the copper wire battery he had built in place lay neatly in a row, like sleeping soldiers. He had everything he needed, and if he was successful, tomorrow would be his noisiest, most dynamic, most thrilling experiment yet. His cousin Daisy would be impressed.

～

The following morning, Guglielmo rose early, despite not having slept much. He was afire with his vision, but somehow managed to gulp down his breakfast of hot chocolate and fette biscottate. Careful that no one observed him, he ran to the springhouse. The morning was wonderfully cool, with one of those teasing breezes that chilled the nape of his neck. A perfect day for a challenge.

The stream seemed to sing encouragements to him, and the architecture of its rocky banks was a perfect site for his plan. Guglielmo spent all morning setting up his experiment. He lugged the battery out to the stream bank and strung wire between two willow trees. Then he attached each dinner plate to the wire with metal clips. Each plate, with the family crest arranged so the doves appeared to fly away, was suspended above the rocky bank. He was only dimly aware of the stream's lilting tune as it cascaded across the slate and granite stones. He then ran another wire to the suspended wire and laid its end close to the battery. If all went well, the plates would fall on the rocks with a tremendously delicious crash. By midafternoon, he was set. He went to find Daisy.

In her own way, Daisy was as stubborn as her cousin. She was busy making dolls out of hollyhocks and wooden clothespins. She sat in the shade of a chestnut, the garden bumblebees droning as they flew heavily from rose to rose. At first, she refused to come. She had made four dolls and was busy with a fifth. "Why should I?" she asked reasonably.

Guglielmo described what was about to happen. The loud, electric sound, the huge and satisfying crash. If she stayed and made her fifth doll, which she could do at any time, she would miss something that was a first. Something that had not been seen before. Something she would probably never see again. Daisy jumped up, her dolls forgotten.

Back at the stream bank, Guglielmo waited until Daisy was properly seated and comfortable. She smoothed her white muslin dress, put her hands in her lap, and stared up at him. His audience was ready, the equipment was ready, and he was more than ready. He connected the copper wire. The response was instantaneous. A thunderous electrical sound erupted, the plates were released from the wire, and they crashed down on the rocks, breaking into a thousand pieces.

Daisy, after a second of shock, clapped in appreciation. It had been an exciting moment. Guglielmo bowed like a magician, his heart full with his success. It wasn't until he straightened back up that he realized he had more than one audience member. His father stood on the opposite bank, a spaniel at his side. His face was dark, forbidding, terrible.

Summoned to his father's study, Guglielmo stood outside the mahogany door for a moment with his ear against the wood. At least his father wasn't shouting. He entered the room and decided to focus on the painting of hunting dogs above the mantle. A fire was burning, and Guglielmo could see his father's legs peeking out from behind his wingback chair, where he sat waiting.

Guglielmo knew there was no use trying to postpone his punishment. Still, he wasn't prepared for the sound of his father's voice. Void of emotion, icy and sharp, it was a weapon all its own. Giuseppe put heavy emphasis on certain words.

"Do you know what you have done?" he said. "You have *stolen* property that does not belong to you. You have *destroyed* property that does not belong to you. You have destroyed ten emblems of our family, wantonly, without regard. They have been in our family for generations. They are *irreplaceable*. Do you understand? And all in the name of these stupid experiments that consume you.

"Your mother has supported you in your silly games. Well, this stops. This all stops *now*."

Guglielmo was in bed for three days, lying on his stomach. His mother was sad and silent but in constant attendance. His pillows were fluffed, his back was rubbed, and his stomach was full of ribollita, a comforting soup made of bread and vegetables. His backside was bruised and raw from his father's belt, but his mind was bruised the most.

What would happen now? Would his father continue to stand in his way? All during the beating, his father had maintained a cold demeanor and a mechanical hand, which had kept on beating long after Guglielmo ceased to cry out. He would never forget being bent over his father's knee, his face crushed into brown tweed pants that smelled of Toscano cigars. Between blows, he had glimpsed his mother's anxious face peeping from the hallway and heard Daisy's wails from another part of the house.

But even as his Giuseppe continued to punish him, Guglielmo was thinking about ways to circumvent him. Perhaps if he stayed far from the house, he could set up some experiments deep in the woods, where no one was likely to stumble over them. Whatever his father thought of his dinner plate experiment, Guglielmo knew that it had been a crashing success.

Chapter Four

THE METRONOME: 1883

The metronome was ticking and tocking and knocking inside his head. His mother stood before him, her hands on her hips. Guglielmo was seated at the piano, his childish fingers trying valiantly to play the right notes with the right fingers at the right pace. It seemed impossible. Even the arpeggios were difficult. He squirmed, and the piano bench squeaked along the joints. He begged for release. Annie's eyes drilled twin holes. There would be no release today.

Day in and day out, without fail, he practiced. At first, he resented the routine and the dullness of the exercises, but he grew to appreciate the focus and discipline. It was structure, and within the structure there was a certain comfort, a certain knowing. He knew where he would be, what he would be doing, and when he would be doing it. And he was building something. He was growing something.

He started with simple tunes and graduated to arias di bravura, which his mother would sing with a full, bosomy voice. Francesco Maria Veracini's *Amor, dover, rispetto* was one of her favorites, and he learned it by heart to please her.

After they performed it together for family and friends who gathered for Christmas that year, and he looked around at the glowing, appreciative faces, Guglielmo started practicing even harder. Discipline, at least for something he was interested in, became like breathing, and the metronome became his friend.

Chapter Five

TURNING SOMETHING INTO SOMETHING ELSE: 1884

Daisy's sewing machine sat on the table in Guglielmo's bedroom. "Stolen!" it seemed to say. "You have stolen me from your best pal, Daisy! The one who made dandelion chains and put them around your neck. The one who gave you the cherry lollipop straight from her own mouth. The one who baited your hook!"

Guglielmo felt a little bit bad but not bad enough. The sewing machine, with its heavy black iron wheel, had long been a powerful temptation. It seemed to ask, "Why am I a sewing machine? Must I always be a sewing machine? Can't I be something else for a while?"

He had also stolen a few tools from the shop in the stable. Hopefully, Piero would not need them today. They lay neatly beside the sewing machine, waiting for his inspiration. A screwdriver, a wrench, and a pair of pliers. One could do a lot with a few simple stolen tools.

With effort, Guglielmo pulled the table to the middle of the room so he could walk around it. The table legs skittered loudly on the wooden floor and he imagined someone bursting through the door, wondering what mischief he was up to. But no one came. No one interfered. He walked around and around, observing the way the parts of the machine were connected.

There it was: the key. A small bolt near the base. He picked up a small pair of pliers and went to work.

An hour later, the sewing machine was in pieces. He had laid it out like a diagram, the wheel on the far right, the rest spread out to the left. He stared. An hour passed.

There was a circular sense to the machine. A turning connection that drove the needle up and down. What else turned? A wheel. Like the crank on the well outside in the yard. A spit. A spit! That's what it would become. He would have to turn the up-and-down motion of the needle into a strictly turning motion. Easy to do, since that was how the wheel turned anyway.

But first, he needed to find a good iron dowel. Guglielmo knew just where to look. Piero, who not only took care of Villa Griffone's squeaking hinges and loose shingles, was also in charge of the large spit by the barn. Here, the family roasted whole pigs. Onto the long, dowel-like iron spike, they threaded quails, lamb, and an occasional boar that the local hunters brought to trade for wine.

Stealth and speed would be his guides. Closing his bedroom door quietly behind him, Guglielmo started down the back stairs, the ones that led directly outdoors.

The day was overcast, and heat lightning flickered over the vineyard hills. Guglielmo wondered aloud why he couldn't hear any thunder. "Perhaps it's too far away," he surmised. "After all, what would the world be like if you could hear everything all at once, no matter how far away?"

He imagined a dense and complicated symphony of flapping birds, clomping Percherons, rattling wagons, honking geese, singing women, tooting boats, ringing bells, chugging trains; the list went on and on. He realized that he had stopped in the middle of the yard, and he wondered how long he had been standing there, his body arrested by his churning mind.

The air was heavy, weighted down by the stalled storm. Piero was staring at the axle of the hay wagon. He wiped his hands on his pants, smearing them with a line of grease. When he saw Guglielmo, he smiled, his suntanned face wrinkled and worn. He had often helped Guglielmo with small mechanical problems. Which way to turn to loosen a bolt. How to properly hold a hammer. Which screwdriver to use for which screw. He enjoyed teaching, and Guglielmo often wished he could learn more from him, for Piero had the gift of a natural mechanic.

However, Piero would definitely not abet him in dismantling the spit. But he wouldn't need to. Guglielmo realized that the spike was far too heavy for the sewing machine. The scale was off. His eyes rested on one of the screwdrivers Piero had been using. It sat on the black tarp where he put his tools to keep them clean. The screwdriver had replaceable heads that clicked into the handle. The flat head was just the right size for what Guglielmo needed.

Guglielmo had a sudden pang of conscience. If he took the tool, Piero would spend the rest of the day looking for it, trying to remember where he had put it, trying to reconstruct where he had used it last.

Piero stretched, his lanky frame seeming to touch the sky, and claimed the next hour was lunchtime. Guglielmo would have to act fast.

As Piero went to find the lunch that his wife made for him every day, Guglielmo grabbed the screwdriver and fled back to the house. He ran straight into Mignani, the family butler. Tall, gaunt, and dressed in black, Mignani resembled an undertaker. His eyes were those of a hawk. He immediately spied the screwdriver in Guglielmo's hand, as well as his guilty expression. Mignani put his hand out. Guglielmo hid the screwdriver behind his back. Mignani stood there, his age-spotted hand held steadily out in front of him, unfazed. Guglielmo reluctantly gave him the screwdriver and told him he had borrowed it from Piero.

Unbeknownst to Guglielmo, Mignani had been observing him quietly ever since he was born. The boy displayed an uncanny curiosity about the world. Mignani had followed his inquisitive mind, watched him conflict with his father, watched as he was doted on by his mother. He had seen the skinny legs elongate and the skinny ankles poke out from beneath the boy's trousers. Mignani had never married, never had a son. So he watched and loved from afar.

He told Guglielmo not to move—not one inch. He turned, left the room, and came back carrying a shiny new red-handled screwdriver. "This one is yours," he said, briefly laying his hand on the boy's head. At that moment, Mignani became a confidant and a co-conspirator. From that day on, Guglielmo relied on his assistance whenever he could be wrested from his household chores.

Back in his room, Guglielmo separated the screwdriver bit and jury-rigged it onto the mechanism that used to be a sewing machine. He installed the wheel and tinkered with the rest of the machine until he had a working spit. He wished he could try a squab on it. He was sitting back, admiring his new creation, when he felt eyes drilling into his back.

He turned to see Daisy, her mouth set in a frown. "You always do this," she said, "You always take advantage of me and my things and the fact that I won't tell on you. That was a very nice sewing machine I got from Nana, and you have ruined it." Although her words were calm, they had a shivering edge to them, and Guglielmo realized she was close to crying.

Guglielmo felt like a monster. He took a handkerchief out of his pocket and dried the solitary tear that had fallen from Daisy's left eye. He sat her down on the bed and explained what he had done. Then, step by step, he took the spit apart.

When he had everything laid out neatly, he reunited the screwdriver bit with its handle. He began to reconstruct the sewing machine. As he worked, he explained to Daisy what he thought each part was for. Every piece was important and served a function. There was nothing superfluous, nothing extra. The last thing he attached was the brass nameplate saying "Howe Sewing Machine." Even that had a purpose.

To Guglielmo, machines were fascinating. Every bolt, every washer, every piece of metal did something. Useful machines were sparse and to the point. He thought about manufacturing and how much an extra bolt might cost if you were making hundreds of them.

Daisy watched him closely. He demonstrated that her sewing machine was now as good as before. She sniffed, pushed him aside, and was not satisfied until she had run two pieces of white sheeting through it. The needle soundlessly and effortlessly bound them together.

Without saying another word, she left the room and reentered a few minutes later with her wooden wagon. She stood still, her arms folded and her chin jutting out, as Guglielmo muscled the sewing machine into the wagon. When he had finished, Daisy left, pulling the wagon behind her, the wheels squeaking under the unaccustomed weight. She did not speak to him for the rest of the week.

Chapter Six

THE STILL IN THE FOREST: 1886

Guglielmo led Daisy through the bougainvillea, the *Clematis armandii*, the boxwoods, and the junipers. He held her tightly by the hand, aware that she could easily become lost in the thick forest behind the house. She squinted as the sun lost out to the deep shadows.

He came to a stop before a mechanical contraption of tubes and glass that was filled with some kind of liquid. She thought she recognized some of her aunt's best glassware, as well as a few stolen forks. A small fire kept the liquid bubbling slightly.

Guglielmo swept his hand through the air, presenting the device to his favorite cousin. "It's a still!"

"What's a still?" she asked. "Can I put a stick in the fire? Isn't that Zia Annie's best serving fork? What's that bubbling noise? I think I smell something funny. Isn't Zio Giuseppe going to be angry?"

"Father will never hear about this," Guglielmo said firmly, pretending to zip up Daisy's lips.

"Will you play *Strega Ghiaccio* with me?" she said, losing interest.

"I don't want to be the Ice Witch, and you are too young to be the Ice Witch. Besides, we need more kids to play. Pay attention, Daisy. Can you keep this a secret?"

She looked at him with a hurt expression. "Haven't I kept the rest of them? The time you sat in the oil paints—did I say anything?" There was a whisper of laughter around her mouth.

She was referring to the day Guglielmo had sat on her palette of oil paints. He was wearing summer whites. As they tried to clean up the mess with turpentine, the noon lunch bell rang. To be late for a meal, any meal, was to face his father's disapproval or rage. Guglielmo was on time for lunch, but the turpentine began to burn him. He tried to ignore it by naming all the Greek gods in his head, but he was sitting in a pool of fire.

"Pass the *patate al forno*, please," he remembered Daisy saying with a smile. "Isn't this a beautiful day?" He kicked at her under the table but missed. The pain was unbearable. His mother looked at him with a question in her eyes. He began to squirm. He couldn't help it. His pants were saturated with turpentine, and the burning was getting worse. And then, from nowhere, Daisy said, "A chi fa male, mai mancano scuse." (He who does evil, is never short of an excuse.) She began to laugh silently, her shoulders shaking. As she stared down at the table, tears ran down her cheeks.

His father took off his glasses, pierced Guglielmo with a beady, owl-like stare, and growled, "What is going on?" His question propelled Guglielmo to his feet. He could stand it no more. He whispered in his mother's ear. Annie jumped up, excused them both from the table, and took him out of the room. She brought him immediately to a bathroom, filled the tub with water, and plunged him in, clothes and all. Guglielmo had never felt such relief.

After his experience, he was so curious about turpentine that he went to his father's library and looked it up. He was amazed that turpentine oil was used for some ailments. Imagine applying that hideous burning liquid to your skin by choice.

Daisy had a stick and was poking the fire with one end. "Well, if you don't want to play games, what do you want to do?" Guglielmo wanted to explain the still to her. He was proud of knowing things, and every day he knew more. He collected ideas like some children collected tadpoles and fireflies.

Guglielmo thought back on the day when he discovered his father's huge library. It was in the northwest corner of the house, on the first floor. It was cool and dark and filled with massive leather chairs and floor-to-ceiling bookcases. The windows were covered with dark red velvet curtains. In the summer, when the light threatened to sear the backs of your eyes, you could go there and pretend it was your own private cave.

On his first visit, Guglielmo found a small red book embossed with gold letters. It was about Ben Franklin and the storm, the key, and the kite. Guglielmo sat down in one of the chairs, which swallowed his body with a sigh, and opened the book. He was completely lost in the story when his father entered. The elder Marconi grabbed his son by the arm and pulled him from the chair so hard that Guglielmo thought his muscles would tear in half. He was booted out with no words and no ceremony—but not before he had stuffed the book down the back of his pants.

After hiding the book under his pillow, Guglielmo went straight to his mother. She was in her private drawing room on the second floor, with walls painted Venetian yellow and diaphanous teal sheers that floated in even a slight breeze. Seeing his face, white and stiff, she put down her mending and asked what was wrong.

His complaint poured out in a torrent of grief. To be kicked out of a place that held so much for him was unbearable. He knew that each book held worlds, people, places, inventions, history, and most of all, ideas. Knowledge he craved but didn't yet have.

Annie patted her son gently on the hand, but Guglielmo could feel her starting to boil and burn under her fair skin. This was something that mattered greatly to her son. She would see it mended as easily as the stocking she had set aside.

It was a war Giuseppe couldn't win. Annie, with her Irish temper leading the way, found her husband in the fields, tying up grapevines. She marched directly toward him, lifting her dark skirts above the mud. Once she began talking, it was hard to hear when she took a breath, for she went on for ten whole minutes.

Giuseppe stood silently, the clouds building at first behind his eyes. But gradually, as Annie wound down, he calmed down as well. By the time she stopped, his response was almost reasonable.

Later, he sat Guglielmo down and lectured him about the worth of books. How invaluable they were. How vulnerable and delicate they were. How they should never be left out in the rain, or forgotten at a friend's house. How one should never dog-ear a page or write in a book or damage a book in any way. Then Giuseppe used the occasion to harp on something else that bothered him. Perhaps, he suggested, reading would improve his son's Italian. Like many people who were raised with more than one language, Guglielmo spoke both English and Italian with an accent, which rankled his father.

Guglielmo seemed to be at rapt attention, but his mind was on the book beneath his pillow. After what felt like an eternity,

Giuseppe tired of talking. Guglielmo excused himself and shot back upstairs to his room.

He read the book all night. He turned the gas down when people went by so they wouldn't see the light under his door. After midnight, when the household had settled down, Guglielmo was in 1752. The air crackled with electricity, and the storm was beginning to howl. Ben Franklin hadn't told anyone but his son, William, what he was planning to do, but he had a theory that lightning was an electrical phenomenon, and he was going to prove it by flying a kite.

Earlier that day, the story went, Ben and William made a kite from a square of silk and two sticks. They tied one end of a silk thread to the kite and an iron key to the other. Then Ben tied a white silk ribbon to the key. He knew that playing with electricity was like playing with fire, and the ribbon would act as insulation. The two Franklins took a thin metal wire and attached the key to a device called a Leyden jar.

Guglielmo lapped up the scientific details like a cat laps up milk.

The Leyden jar was invented by a man named Ewald Georg von Kleist in 1745. He was experimenting with electricity when he accidently touched his electrical generator to a nail stuck in the cork of a bottle. Several hours later, he touched the nail and received a hefty shock. The jar had stored the electricity.

Kleist did not get credit for this amazing discovery. Instead, a man named Pieter van Musschenbroek, from a small town in Holland called Leiden, received the fame. He made the same discovery later than Kleist, but he communicated it at the right time to the right people. Guglielmo made a mental note of that.

The Franklins managed to get the kite up in the stormy skies. It bucked and tossed in the strong winds, and Ben, who was staying dry in a barn, held onto the white ribbon with difficulty. Guglielmo imagined the disaster if the knots hadn't held. The experiment would have been a bust. Someone else might have gotten the credit.

Before Ben touched the key, it gave him a good, strong shock. If it hadn't, it might have killed him. Even as he automatically jerked his hand back, he started to smile. He and William began to laugh in exhilaration. There could no longer be any doubt. Lightning contained electricity! Franklin went on to invent lightning rods, the Franklin stove, the glass harmonica, bifocals, and the odometer.

The cocks were crowing when Guglielmo finished the book. He lay in bed with his arms behind his head. He knew what he wanted to be. An inventor. And he knew what he wanted to invent. Or at least what he wanted to invent with. Electricity thrilled him. It was the stuff of dreams, the material of science. He would engage in his own experiments. He would fly his own kites. People would remember the name of Marconi.

Daisy jerked him back to the forest, the still, and the faintly medicinal smell of alcohol. She was brandishing the burnt end of the stick alarmingly close to his nose. "Tyger, tyger burning bright," she chanted. "In the forests of the night."

Guglielmo shouted at her. "Stop, Daisy before someone gets burned! Like me!"

"What are you going to do with this, anyway?" she asked. "A still isn't good for anything."

"It's good for making alcohol," Guglielmo said. He cocked his head, waiting for her to be impressed. And she was. She had seen how silly adults became after having too much alcohol. It was like a magic potion that turned adults from serious, concerned, and scolding parents, to carefree, jiggly, stumbling people.

Guglielmo let her try a small sample of the clear liquid that was dripping from a copper tube into a bottle. She sputtered, choked, and spit. How could people stand such a taste? It burned all the way down. Daisy thought she could feel a thin strip of fire from her throat to her stomach.

A small cough nearby. Guglielmo heard it through the forest birds and rustling leaves. He turned to see his mother standing there, holding a basket filled with flowers. He suddenly felt as though he was in the Roma Termini railway station. The forest felt crowded with people. How had his mother found him? Annie set the basket down, put her hands on her hips, and surveyed the scene.

A wren sang in an elder tree, and the sedge grasses rustled. It was a beautiful day with a breeze that carried the slight scent of alcohol to her nose. This smell was no stranger to her, for she had grown up a Jameson of the Jameson Irish Whiskey family. The distillation of alcohol had made her family's fortune. She sat down on the grass.

"I think I see my best serving fork," she said. Guglielmo stared at the ground. "Also some of my canning jars, and copper tubing that, if I'm not mistaken, went missing from Piero's workbench." She clicked her tongue against the roof of her mouth. "You have a wonderful mind, *cucciolo*, but thievery is a very bad thing. If you go on like this, poor Maria will have nothing to cook with and we will have nothing to eat, because you will have stolen everything away for your experiments. "

Guglielmo concentrated on the ground, where an ant was trying to lift a leaf twice its size. "I will tell you what we are going to do. Daisy, I want you to go get your wagon. Say nothing to anyone." Without a word, Daisy left, eager to escape the lecture. "Guglielmo, I hope you have your tools, because you are going to dismantle this still and return every single thing to its proper place."

"Will you tell father?" Guglielmo whispered the words, dreading her response.

"I see no reason why I should," she replied. "He will only misunderstand your intentions. If you do as I say and put every bolt back, I will spare you the embarrassment. Now let's talk about how much sugar and yeast you started with."

Guglielmo enjoyed telling his mother his scientific methodology. Annie had a fine mind, and having been raised in the family business, she knew a few things about how to make alcohol. For her, this was revisiting her upbringing, being in the room when the adults began talking about residual sugars and bottle shapes. For Guglielmo, it was an opportunity to share his thinking.

This particular endeavor had combined chemistry, mechanics, ingenuity, problem-solving, and—his mother reminded him—thievery and subterfuge. But it was during this incident and conversation that she, like Mignani earlier, became a co-conspirator. They had always been close, but forever after, she would be his greatest advocate.

Chapter Seven

MOTHER KNOWS BEST: 1887

It is a time-honored tradition: the new boy always gets pillo-ried. After years of informal education, Guglielmo had finally become a formal student. His father had insisted, deciding that Guglielmo, consumed by his small and silly experiments, badly needed discipline and structure. Annie tried to intervene, saying that schools were run by idiots who tried to stamp out the genius in young boys. But this time, Giuseppe prevailed. Guglielmo was now enrolled at the Istituto Cavallero in Florence.

His mother firmly believed that education, great education, included stepping out of the way of children's true curious nature. She herself had experienced an end to joyful learning at the hands of a strict and rigid series of teachers at a finishing school for young ladies in Sutton. She used to think wryly of the term "finishing" and reflected that it had almost finished her.

It was only through music that Annie could intellectually fly. When she was singing, she was free from constraints. When she sang a coloratura, the intricate notes flowed from her like water out of a spring. Her mind soared, her imagination ran free, and anything was possible.

She wanted that freedom for her favorite child, for she recognized that Guglielmo was not like other children. There was something about the way his mind worked, the way it moved constantly from topic to topic, the way it connected the dots, that could not be lost or stamped on. She knew that adults frequently interrupted the flow of young minds, and she believed that often the best thing for grown-ups to do was nothing.

And yet Guglielmo found himself in the front of his new class, holding an open book, his new schoolmaster standing beside him with a dowel in one hand and a ruler in the other. He was twelve. He was supposed to begin reading in Italian, a language he was not fluent in.

Perhaps his inability traced back to a tyrannical grammar school instructor named Germano Bollini, who had attempted to pound the language into his head. Sometimes, when Guglielmo was seated at the table with Bollini, he pictured a huge castle door complete with a giant iron ring and rusted hasps. At the beginning of the lesson, the door was open, but soon it would slam shut with a deafening clang, and Guglielmo would learn no more that day.

Guglielmo stood in front of his classmates, something he had not experienced before. He gazed at them and recognized expressions of arrogance, greed, and meanness. Like sharks swimming around shipwreck victims, they were watching for weakness and the first signs of blood.

The schoolmaster was part of this hazing ritual. Through thin lips under a pencil moustache, he said, "Your Italian is atrocious. You speak like a foreigner. Now read the Manzoni poem you have been studying. And speak up!"

Guglielmo began slowly. "He was: and motionless in death. As that unconscious clay. Robbed of —" He was drowned out by howls of derision. He glanced sideways at the teacher, expecting him to stop the ruckus, then realized this was part of the educational process.

The teacher looked at him smugly, his thoughts written clearly on his face. "Teasing and mocking is an educational impetus," Guglielmo read in his teacher's expression. "This will make the boy learn. This is a day the boy will remember, and it will make him try harder."

Guglielmo struggled to hold back his tears. If he cried, he would forever be that boy—weak. A sissy. A *donnicciola*. He thought about his experiments and his private successes. The sting behind his eyes stopped. He took on a haughty expression. He would not bow under this peer pressure. He would stand tall. He envisioned the oak that stood behind his house. He would be like that: able to withstand terrible storms and high winds. He stood perfectly still in the rain of hoots and screams of laughter. Without moving a muscle, he looked out at his classmates with a serious, superior eye. He stared them down, and one by one, they fell silent.

His education would continue like that until the Marconis left Florence and moved to one of Guglielmo's favorite towns: Livorno.

One can look back on one's childhood and see moments when life shifts and everything changes. Guglielmo's enrollment at the Istituto Tecnico in Livorno was one of those shifts.

Even Giuseppe eventually recognized that the Florence school was not a good fit for his son. The hazing had a negative impact on Guglielmo, who became more solitary, reluctant to participate in family outings, and even to come to the dinner table. When he did make an appearance, he was silent, staring at his plate, eating more out of habit than joy, and leaving as soon as he was able.

Annie was heartbroken. The light of her brilliant boy was being extinguished.

She prevailed on Giuseppe to act, and for once, he agreed with her. They enrolled Guglielmo in a school tailored for boys who were interested in the physical world. They were tinkerers, mathematicians, biologists. They wanted to build buildings. This was a school Guglielmo could dive into.

He now found himself sitting in the front row of a large lecture hall. His pad of paper was open on the desk, ready to receive every word of his new hero, Professor Giotto Bizzarrini, who was lecturing on a relatively new topic called physics.

Guglielmo learned about Nicolas Léonard Sadi Carnot, who experimented with heat and energy, and about the first law in thermodynamics—the law of the conservation of energy. He learned that light travels more slowly in water; that gases are made of molecules in constant motion; that when watching a waterwheel carefully, one could see something called the Coriolis effect.

He could not get enough. It was as if the castle door that had once slammed shut flew open again. New ideas flooded his mind. He clamored for more. He was insatiable and pestered his mother for other educational opportunities.

Annie arranged for Guglielmo to be privately tutored by a man he came to adore: Professor Vincenzo Rosa, who taught at the Liceo Niccolini, a high school known for its humanistic approach to education. Rosa was a man who lived and breathed the transferal of knowledge. Childless, he was married to his job of instilling in his students a clear, concise methodology. He was rigorous without being pedantic, serious without losing the excitement of learning.

Guglielmo could now add a dash of process to his already burgeoning stew of talents. He began to see how science was a language, a way to proceed. It was a little like how Maria made her famous cakes. She had an idea about her next creation, she gathered her ingredients, and she made careful notations as she went along. If the cake was not quite right, she would vary only one element the next time, to see if that made the cake worse or better.

Guglielmo realized that Maria was a kind of scientist, and he vowed to bring her a rose the next time he saw her.

Guglielmo sat in the stiff, overstuffed sitting room belonging to one of the many families his mother knew. He smelled the pink roses on the table, the faint loam of English Breakfast tea, and the slight tang of lemon slices. He stared at the girl who sat across from him. She was blond. Her hair was still in braids. She was sixteen. She stared back at him as she stirred two lumps of sugar into her tea. Her name was Margherita Sarfatti. Guglielmo was in awe.

For two weeks, the smell of Venice became intricately tied with the roses, the tea, the lemon, and the beauty of Margherita. The adults spun around them in orbits. There were a few parties, several dinners, and a breakfast or two. She always seemed to be within a few feet of him. She had a peculiar habit of fanning herself, even when there was a cool breeze, and the wry smile she gave him made him think she knew something he did not.

It would be years before he met her again, and in very different circumstances, but he would never forget her painted fan with its small red flowers, nor the roses, the tea, the lemon.

Chapter Eight

PLAYING WITH POSEIDON: 1888

It was a sticky summer day, the air barely moving, Villa Griffone the only cool refuge for miles. Even the chickens, who usually jittered and clucked, looking for worms, were inside their coop, seeking relief from the heat. Guglielmo had gotten up early, taken one step outside, and retreated to the library, trying to stay as still as possible.

He sat at a table with a stack of books on Greek mythology, poring through them, one after another, meandering, stopping to let a story soak in. He was interrupted by Justina, one of the maids. She had come to fetch him for his father, who wanted to speak with him.

Fourteen-year-old Guglielmo mentally went through all the crimes he might need to account for, but he came up empty. Being summoned by his father was potentially negative, for Giuseppe was not involved in the daily raising of his children, unless a disciplinary action was needed. Had Guglielmo forgotten something? He watched as Justina left the room. He had never noticed the saucy brown curl on the nape of her neck.

Soon he was rapping on his father's door. Giuseppe commanded him to enter.

Guglielmo smelled the cigar smoke and the faint traces of last night's wine. The clock on the mantel with its sweet tick and dissonant tock was the only thing he could hear. No voices from the outside, none from the kitchen. It was as though just the two of them existed in the entire world.

His father sat near the window, his craggy face bifurcated by a sliver of light that sliced through the darkness of the room. Guglielmo approached slowly, not sure what was coming next but assuming the worst. History had made him a leery guest in his father's study.

Giuseppe rose, gestured with his crooked index finger, and silently led him to the backyard. The sun was brutal, hammering them both as they stepped outside. Giuseppe crossed to the hay barn, slid open the huge double door, and entered the relatively cool interior.

The barn felt like the Grotta del Cavallone, a cave in Abruzzo, which the family had visited once. Guglielmo remembered Daisy falling against a stalagmite and chipping it off as she grabbed for balance. The straw caught between the cracks of the hay mound made him think of the stalactites that hung from the cave's ceiling. You could remember which one was which, because stalactites with a C were the ones that hung from the ceiling, and stalagmites with a G were the ones that came up from the ground. He wondered why they didn't have the same root word.

He sneezed. The particulate matter in the air of the barn always had that impact on him. His nose started running and he reached for a handkerchief. Why had his father brought him here? It took a moment for his eyes to adjust to the darkness. Something large and white appeared in the gloom. He felt his father's heavy hand on his shoulder and resisted the temptation to shudder out from under it.

"It's yours," his father said, gesturing expansively with his other arm. Guglielmo's brain finally comprehended what he was looking at. A slim, freshly painted sailboat with "Sognare" written on the side. A word that meant "to dream." Guglielmo knew he would.

Daisy and Guglielmo sailed every day that summer. The Marconis were staying on the Viale Regina Margherita in Livorno at the Palace Hotel, a four-story, high-class Italian establishment with every comfort, suitable for a lengthy stay. The hotel was popular with the Italian elite, who often came there to escape the heat. The bay breezes freshened the air and kept it crisp.

A line of poplars and a single street were all that separated them from the Ligurian Sea. The *Sognare* was tied up at the cement pier, along with other small sailing boats, and Guglielmo could see it from his bedroom window, which faced the bay. He and Daisy would rush to the kitchen, pack a lunch of bread, olive oil, and salami, stuff some extra clothes into a drawstring bag, and take off before the adults were awake.

As the *Sognare* sliced through the turquoise seawater, Guglielmo was free to let his mind roam. He thought about the conductive powers of saltwater and wondered why drinking water didn't conduct electricity at all. He thought about the Ligurian Sea and how it links up with the Mediterranean Sea and the Tyrrhenian Sea and wondered where, exactly, one sea changed from one to the other. Was there a distinct point? A longitudinal or latitudinal line?

Daisy was interested in fish, and she always carried at least one identification book, in case they brought up something strange when they dropped anchor and their fishing lines. They had brought up breams, bass, pandoras, monkfish, anchovies, and rock mullets. Daisy would pull out her paints, do a quick sketch, and apply a dash of watercolors before their colors began to fade. She always felt a bit sad at that moment, watching as their eyes turned milky, but Guglielmo was thinking about the colors and why they were fading, and what made them fade, and if he could ever invent something that would prevent them from fading, and whether that would make him any money.

However, his favorite thing to do was to cross in front of the navy boats. This habit of Guglielmo's put Daisy into a constant state of terror. The *Regia Marina Castore* (Castor) and *Polluce* (Pollux) gunboats patrolled the Ligurian Sea and docked only a few kilometers from where they kept the *Sognare*. Whenever possible, he would tack in front of them, snubbing all marine protocols of right-of-way.

The sailors, scarcely older than Guglielmo, came to play a part in the game. They would seem to veer toward him, threatening to crush his smaller boat with their iron prows. Their top speed was eight knots, his own top speed, but he was a swallow to their albatrosses. Capitalizing on the constant breezes that came down from the north, he could swoop and cavort in front of them. Daisy, gripping the rails so hard her hands hurt, didn't think this was a particularly beneficial way to spend time, but Guglielmo enjoyed the heart-pounding rush.

His intense love of the sea would never leave him. Indeed, it would become a crucial drive in his future.

Chapter Nine

THE FIRST LAB: 1888

Guglielmo tugged impatiently on his mother's hand, her wedding ring digging into his palm. He threw the door open to the third-floor attic. There, dusted by age, were the feeding trays, the glass worm containers, and the larger bottles for the moths. His grandfather had raised silkworms in the attic, which still smelled faintly of mulberry leaves. Guglielmo, his eyes watching his mother's face intently, declared, "This is my new laboratory!"

Annie drew a handkerchief from her sleeve and blew the dust from her nose. The old attic room was unused and forgotten, but she knew that it still represented a coming battle. Giuseppe would put up some kind of roadblock. How to deal with Guglielmo was the one thing she and her husband always disagreed on. She stepped inside and looked around.

The windows were covered with grime that filtered the light like thick gauze. The tables were rough, probably hand-built by her father-in-law from pines felled in the surrounding hills.

It was perfect.

～

Annie waited until Giuseppe had finished his after-dinner port. She peeped through the half-open door of the drawing room and watched as he filled his pipe, smoked it, and set it down on the tray beside his chair. She saw him take his shoes off and put his feet up on the needlepoint ottoman. He was as relaxed as he would ever be.

She swept into the room in her rose-colored moiré silk dress. It shimmered like water in the gaslight. She knew it was his favorite. She sat down in the companion chair, her customary chair, and picked up her latest needlepoint project, a single iris in a bed of daisies. The only sounds in the room were the snapping of the fire, an occasional crumbling when a log fell apart, and the hiss of the gaslights. She sighed, knowing the sound would echo through the room like a thunderclap in a cave.

Giuseppe, his head at a tilt, looked over his spectacles at her but said nothing. She sighed again. He picked up a book and opened it, but she could see that he wasn't reading. It took one more sigh before he slammed the book shut and threw his glasses down on the table.

This time, he was the one who sighed.

"What is it now, Annie?" he asked. He sounded resigned but not angry.

"It's Guglielmo. He needs space." She kept her voice low and quiet, so the words seemed as light as feathers.

Giuseppe let out a snort, a bolt of sound. "He has the entire outdoors! Miles and miles of streams and fields and hills and groves, and the entire country of God at his disposal! What more could he want?"

"Well, he needs a space where he can have control over wind and rain. He needs to be able to have a table rabbits won't run over at night. He needs a place where he can work for hours on something, put it down overnight, and know it will be there in the morning." She spoke gently. Reaching over, she placed her hand on her husband's wrist.

"But there's no room in this house," Giuseppe protested. "The servants have their spaces, we have ours, and the rest is taken up with storage. We are up to our eaves with people and things and your collection of teapots and —"

"Don't begin on me about those teapots!" she exclaimed, pouncing like a cat on a mouse. "If I could chuck out your gun collection, I would. I'd throw them all down the well. And what about your dogs? I love dogs, but you bring in those four hounds at all hours, and their paws muddy the floors, and they smell like, well, wet dogs when you bring them in out of the rain. But do I complain? No, I do not. And once they come in, they lie around like three-year relatives—you can't move them. And I step over them with full tea trays. So don't talk to me about teapots!" Giuseppe watched her stab at her needlepoint, as if she was stabbing him.

"I guess a few teapots don't matter in the grand scheme of things," he said grudgingly, picking up his pipe in case he needed to defend himself.

"No, you really cannot even see them through the dog hair that is constantly floating through the air. Sasha never complains, but I see her pulling it out of the mops with her bare hands."

"I trust you already have a room picked out?" Giuseppe said, getting back to the subject.

"The silkworm room. It has not been used since your father died, and it is perfect for Guglielmo." She finished the last purple stitch on the iris, knotted it, and clipped it with precision.

Giuseppe considered her proposal. It was true. The room had not been used for years. Not since his father had been found dead in his bed, his face peaceful, his body cold and already almost rock hard. The servants had cleaned the room of the silkworms, taking the jars downstairs and releasing the little creatures into the fields. He wondered briefly if any had survived such a brutal shift in their environs. He envisioned them crawling away in the dust, their white bodies taking on a dusky brown, and wondered if they ate grape leaves.

His mind came back to the decision at hand. Because it was in his nature, he tried to think of all the reasons to say no. He found none.

Annie smiled, understanding that his silence was a victory. She stood and circled around his chair, embraced him from behind. She kissed him lightly on the forehead, which was cool and smelled vaguely of walnuts and summer. She had always loved the way he smelled.

He reached up and pulled the pins from her hair. Her luxurious red hair cascaded down around her face and spilled onto Giuseppe's shoulders. Tonight, they would both win.

Annie looked around the attic room and immediately started thinking about which servants would be best deployed to this dirty task. When she and Guglielmo started rolling up their sleeves at the same time, they laughed. They were a formidable team.

The day became a contest to see who could clean more. Sasha, almost as wide as she was tall, was the mop master, carrying out bucket after bucket of dirty water. Piero was conscripted to repair some of the tables, and Mignani moved whatever someone pointed at. Annie and Guglielmo worked on the windows, cleaning them so the hills, covered with rows of grapevines, planted in military precision, could be clearly seen.

By the end of the day, the room was ready. Annie went off to bed. Guglielmo did not stop until the morning sun touched the windows, reminding him that sleep was a necessity. He had spent the night carrying up the things he would need. Raw materials he had been storing in out-of-the-way corners in the barns, the sheds, the springhouse, and his bedroom. Metal tubes, a hammer, wiring, a pair of rusty pliers, several blocks of oak, three clamps, a vise that had been thrown out because it lacked a threaded rod. Lubricating oil, several squares of cloth, five clothespins, tin snips, two screwdrivers.

Looking around, he saw that his amassed materials were a drop in the bucket. He would need so many more things. Tools to shave metal filings, much more wire, wire cutters. He patted his pockets, wishing that money would magically fill them. How was he going to manage this? The trick was to take things that wouldn't be missed, but he knew that would be difficult. Every tool, every scrap of material was attached to a person.

By now, his laboratory was filled with light. Guglielmo took one last look around before closing the door and going off to bed. His mind was tracing dotted lines to the things he would need. In his cousin's sewing basket was a good pair of scissors. Hanging from the wall in Piero's tool shed was a coiled length of twenty-gauge wire.

Back to money. The problem was money. Most of the materials he needed simply could not be found at home. He had already begged, borrowed, and, to the outrage of almost everyone in the household, stolen everything he could. His father had told him that if he were ever again caught stealing, he would be turned out of the house with his portmanteau and his two pairs of shoes and left sitting in the dusty road.

Shoes! Now that was a thought. Raphael, the boy who lived a half mile down the road, had admired his. And he was a boy with money. He always had at least a few lire in his pocket and could pay for as many Galatines as he wanted when they went to Tito's candy store in Palermo.

Forgetting sleep, Guglielmo set off down the road, his second pair of shoes tucked under his arm, to call on his friend Raphael. Raphael lived in Villa Montalvo, a three-story, mustard-colored stucco house surrounded by tall yew trees. His father was a successful fisherman who owned two fishing boats that came in every day laden with glistening, flapping fish.

Once, Guglielmo had spent the day on one of the boats with Raphael and five fishermen who chewed cheroots, spit, and swore upon their mothers' graves. It had been a great day, with Raphael spinning stories and making up fantastic lies, for all he wanted to be was an author. Thanks to the many days Guglielmo had spent sailing, he did not suffer from seasickness. He stood in the prow, helping Raphael make up stories about pirates, trunks of rubies and diamonds, and women with low-cut dresses. When the main net was drawn in, the winches squealing, and the bulging, shimmering net spilled its contents into the dark hold, Guglielmo thought briefly about becoming a fisherman. He would smell of fish but have the money to buy what he needed to be a great inventor.

Guglielmo's visit with Raphael was successful. He was down to one pair of shoes, but in his pocket were 10,000 lire, enough to buy metal, wire, and batteries. That night, he smoothed the bills flat and slid them beneath his pillow. Perhaps they would affect his dreams and allow his inventions to solidify into real money.

That night, he dreamed about his father. He marched down to his father's den and flung the door open so wide it banged against the walls. He saw his father's frowning face hanging in the middle of the room like a frightening balloon. He emptied so many bags of money onto the table that the coins bounced off the table and rolled all over the floor. His father's eyes grew as wide as the coins themselves. He opened his arms and Guglielmo fell into them like a drowning sailor.

He woke with a start and tears sprang to his eyes. The chances of that dream ever happening were as likely as a rabbit tearing the head off a bear. He thrust his hands under his pillow and, reassuring himself with the feel of the money, fell back asleep.

The next day, when his mother found out what Guglielmo had done, she vowed that she would make sure he always had enough money to do what he needed to do. Annie had her ways of getting what she wanted.

He had been waiting for just such a storm. A slowly building, heavy with the promise of rain storm. He stuck his head out of his laboratory window and adjusted the lightning rod. The metal was cooling off in the quickening winds. He could feel the storm approaching. A voluminous cumulonimbus cloud hung in the sky beyond the hill. Cumulonimbus clouds were the best and most likely to produce the lightning he so needed.

It had been hot, so hot the dogs lay in the shadows. The heat had driven the cloud to form tall drifts, and it was now a towering mass. Rain began to spatter down, large drops that dotted the dusty yard below. He ducked inside and, using a wooden stick, adjusted the coherer, a glass tube filled with metal filings. The thunderhead broke in half with a bolt of sizzling lightning. Guglielmo felt like Benjamin Franklin. The lightning flashed, the battery gathered the electricity, the slender metal filings in the coherer made a neat connection within the tube, and the bell rang.

Chapter Ten

DAISY AND BLOOD: 1888

Daisy felt a bit guilty. She was an accomplice, a co-conspirator. She had sneaked into her aunt's sewing room, found the pink and pearl sewing basket, and pilfered the scissors, all while Maria scrubbed at a spot near the hearth. Daisy was becoming an adroit thief.

She carried the scissors up to her cousin's lab, where even though the sun was scarcely up over the hill, Guglielmo was already at his workbench. Perhaps he had never left, she thought, as she looked at the half-eaten tray of food near his elbow. She brought out the scissors that she had hidden in her pocket. Without a word, he took them and began cutting wire.

Guglielmo, his brow wrinkling in concentration, complained about the quality of the scissors. He needed the wire snips that Piero kept on the wall of the shed. Piero was proud of his tools and had painted silhouettes on the shed wall so each tool could be placed on the same nail every time. The wire snips went missing too often, and Piero finally brought the issue to his father.

As usual, his father reacted with his characteristic rage. Guglielmo envisioned him as a steam engine, his face bulging, steam coming out of his ears, his hair sticking out at all angles. Although the image was funny, the emotion was not, and he needed to stay as far from that anger as possible. Hence, he was using sewing scissors.

Finally, Guglielmo had established neat piles of wire, each pile arranged according to length. His hands ached. "These are terrible scissors, hardly better than using my teeth," he said, opening and closing his hands.

Daisy sat perched on the hard wooden stool. "Get your own scissors next time," she said. She squirmed. "I'm uncomfortable." She had been sitting there the whole time, thinking about her butterflies. She often came to watch her cousin work, preferring his company to that of her more frivolous sisters. She was a budding biologist and kept detailed field notes of the insects and flowers she found. When she wasn't peering through a magnifying glass at her carpenter bees, Italian stinkbugs, and Cleopatra butterflies, she watched Guglielmo tinker with his metal filings and wires. They had formed a close bond, both fascinated by the physical world, each engaged in an active pursuit to learn more about it.

"Then go," he said, gesturing toward the door. "I have important work to do." Pouting, Daisy stared at the back of his head. He was often like this—filled with his own important work. He had a certain concentration that she envied. He would get up early in the morning and be hard at work before sunrise. Sometimes he didn't sleep at all but worked throughout the night. He ignored hunger and other bodily functions. From the smell that came from one corner of the room, she suspected he kept a pee pot so he would not have to leave his precious lab and break his concentration.

Sometimes Daisy tried to tease him away from his work by suggesting they go fishing. In the past, they had enjoyed fishing from the banks of the Savena. They would settle under the willow trees and cast their lines, waiting for a bass to dart out from beneath the rocky bank and strike at a worm on their hooks. She missed those lazy afternoons, the doves asleep in the afternoon haze, the water catching the light so it reflected like diamonds on them both.

Sitting on the river's banks, they discussed why spiders had eight legs, what kind of viper had the most poisonous bite, where birds sheltered during torrential rain. When they were younger, she stripped dandelion stalks, dropped them into the water, and watched them curl. He questioned what made them curl. The shape of the stalks? The long threads that made up the stalks? When she held the dandelion under his chin, saw the warm yellow reflection, and commented that he must love butter, he laughed and tickled her.

But those days were long past. Guglielmo was now a boy obsessed. She suspected much of his drive came from the need to prove himself to her uncle. This was a time-honored theme. From Homer to Shakespeare, men had driven themselves into sharp rocks, taken on immense armies, and killed the people they loved, all for their fathers' approval, which most would never get. Daisy's own father was rarely present, and she lived in a world of women, her mother and sisters surrounding her like moths around a lamp. She preferred the world of boys, but the rough relationship Guglielmo had with his father was not something she envied.

As Daisy stood up to leave, Guglielmo yelped suddenly. She turned to see bright red blood seeping out from under his hands. Together, they stanched the bleeding with the crisp white napkin that lay unused beside the half-eaten bowl of *maccu*, a thick Sicilian soup. Once the bleeding had subsided, they risked peeking at the wound. He had cut off the tip of his ring finger.

"I'll get it stuck back on by and by," he said. "The chemist is not far from here." With a reassuring smile, he went back to work. Daisy left him alone in his lab and went out into the sunshine to see the day unfold.

Chapter Eleven

Guglielmo walked into the darkened room. It was always like this. Nello Marchetti didn't need to see to survive. He didn't need to see to pour his tea or cut up his *arrosto di Agnello*, a roasted leg of lamb he usually had on Sundays. For he was, as Guglielmo put it, "skillfully blind."

Being with Nello was like putting sight away in a cupboard and letting the other senses step forward. Today, the room smelled of cold stone and faded tobacco, with just a hint of dust. Guglielmo could hear the street outside—a child laughing, the crush and squeal of carts going by. A vender selling strawberries, singing his phrase over and over, a repetitive recitative.

Nello greeted him with a slight whistle, a habit Guglielmo found endearing. Guglielmo went to the window and pushed aside the heavy damask curtains to let some light into the room. It was enough to read by. Nello sat on his cracked leather chair, waiting expectantly. His gray hair was parted unevenly down one side, his face badly shaven, his eyes a filmy white. His hands were his grace. They were clasped together like two children in church, waiting expectantly.

"Does George die today?" Nello asked. "Let's find out." Guglielmo had read ahead in the story of Richard III and knew that George had indeed died, brutally assassinated in the Tower of London. He plunged into the world of England and the War of the Roses, and the two of them stayed there for several hours. By the time Guglielmo finished reading, George was dead, and so were the two unfortunate princes.

They agreed that Richard III was a fabulous monster. They talked about the assassinations, the assignations, and the intrigue. The brutality of a powerful man, and whether absolute power did truly corrupt absolutely. They shared a board filled with slabs of rye bread, cheese, and a cluster of green grapes.

Finally, Nello went to the southern windows, still darkened by curtains, and drew them aside. There, between two pots of red geraniums, was a telegraphist's key. With its metal shaft and handle, the device looked a bit like a boot punch and was moored to a block of wood. Standing in the shaft of sunlight, Nello began to use it, tapping out Morse code for Guglielmo to decipher.

S-O-M-E-O-N-E S-H-O-U-L-D H-A-V-E S-K-E-W-E-R-E-D R-I-C-H-A-R-D T-H-E- T-H-I-R-D L-O-N-G A-G-O

Guglielmo took a turn.

Y-E-S W-I-T-H H-I-S O-W-N S-W-O-R-D

It was slow going, and he was just beginning to have some facility. It was like so many things—one had to hammer away, day after day. He needed to practice until he could hear it in his head before going to sleep.

Since he first started learning Morse code from Nello, Guglielmo would sink into the goose down and sing himself to sleep, seeing in his mind's eye A = dot dash, B = dash dot dot dot, C = dash dot dash dot. It was better than counting sheep, and he rarely made it to M = dash dash before he was asleep.

Nello tapped out something else.

W-H-A-T M-E-S-S-A-G-E S-H-O-U-L-D T-H-E V-I-C-T-I-M-S H-A-V-E S-E-N-T

Guglielmo knew exactly how to respond.

S-O-S

Dot dot dot, dash dash dash, dot dot dot. This was the first time he had used these three letters, but they would become increasingly important in the years to come.

Chapter Twelve

Alfonso came down the stairs three at a time and rocketed out the front door. Guglielmo was still eating his breakfast, but he knew that love was propelling Alfonso out of the house that morning.

They were summering in the Biellese Alps, and a girl Alfonso was infatuated with was an ardent Catholic. They planned to meet at the Black Madonna in the sanctuary of Oropa. Painted in shining gold gilt and surrounded by golden stars, she was said to have been carved by Saint Luke himself, and thousands made a yearly pilgrimage to see and touch her. The wooden statue had never gotten wormwood; it had never worn down, even though thousands had touched her; and dust never settled on her face or the baby Jesus, who rode on her arm with a big smile.

The girl had promised to hold Alfonso's hand and walk with him to church if he would first meet her at the statue. Guglielmo stirred his eggs around on his plate, lost in thought. Although girls had always been of interest to him, he wasn't sure how far he would go to gain one. Would he pretend to believe something he didn't believe in? Would he ever do something he didn't believe in doing? He needed to get his mind off girls and on to something more productive. He went upstairs to read some of the articles he had brought with him from the University of Bologna.

As he turned the pages of a journal, he stopped suddenly. If he could have, he would have gulped the article down like he was drinking a *limoncello*. He couldn't get the information into his brain fast enough. Here, in Bodoni black type, was Heinrich Rudolf Hertz's proof that electromagnetic waves existed. It was as though someone had opened his head and poured in molten lava, for he was on fire.

All the work of the years before—the patchwork experimentation, the tinkering, the long nights hand-filing metal rods, trying antennas made of metal sheeting and wire—added up to this moment. Guglielmo felt as if he himself had cohered and come into focus. The small metal filings in his mind were finally in alignment. He was electrified.

Hertz had been an amazing scientist, capable in many ways, but Guglielmo thought he lacked imagination. About his discovery, Hertz had said, "It's of no use whatsoever. This is just an experiment that proves Maestro Maxwell was right—we just have these mysterious electromagnetic waves that we cannot see with the naked eye. But they are there." Hertz was referring to English scientist James Clerk Maxwell, who developed a theory to explain electromagnetic waves. It was Hertz who proved they existed. But when asked what they might be used for, Hertz replied, "Nothing, I guess."

Nothing? *Nothing?* Guglielmo couldn't believe what he had just read. Here was a man who had discovered something invisible that no one else could perceive. He had put a name to it. He had proved that these mysterious waves truly existed, and yet he could not imagine an application?

He had proved that a bell could be triggered to ring across a room. And if you could trigger it to ring across a room, why not across the world? And why limit it to just a bell? If Guglielmo could harness this electrical wave, he could it ride it like one of his father's finest stallions. He could make lights turn on in Boston, or a factory in Australia begin its work day, or one of Karl Benz's automobiles start up and take off without anyone in the driver's seat. He could send men to the moon.

Hertz's article had put a match to Guglielmo's mind, and from that moment forward, there was no stopping him.

Chapter Thirteen

THE SHOT: 1895

Guglielmo hadn't slept all night. Too keyed up. Instead, he had envisioned the day, the light winds ushering in fluffy white clouds, the sun warming the black cloth on his back, the moment when he would hear the shot. That moment would be his moment, the day his life truly began.

He had lain awake, his body trembling, his head so full of images that they crowded out any chance of sleep. He tried counting sheep and started thinking about lanolin and wool and where lanolin came from. He tried counting using Fibonacci numbers, but his mind, uncharacteristically difficult to tame, lost interest at 987.

Sometimes he wished that the spinning of the world would stop so the day remained the day and he could work until he dropped, but inevitably the night came with its restriction, its darkness, and its need for gas or kerosene. More than once, his father had caught him working late at night, and he had shouted about Guglielmo wasting oil, wasting time, and wasting his life with these stupid, inane experiments that would go nowhere. His father believed in the red grapes that would produce wine, the golden fields that would produce wheat. He believed in production as a tangible, edible, marketable commodity that you could eat or sell. His father, with his pragmatic belief in produce, could not believe in what Guglielmo was trying to do, and he had no desire to start.

Guglielmo sighed. Thinking about his father was a sure pathway to sleeplessness. He flopped over and buried his head in his pillow.

When morning finally came, it was not as he had imagined it would be. The day was cloudy, almost stormy, with the kind of grayness that seeped into one's mind. As soon as the light crept into his room, Guglielmo was up, throwing on his clothes thoughtlessly, dashing downstairs where all the equipment lay ready by the kitchen door. Maria was already up, making small sighing noises as she worked around the table and the pile of what she called "mechanicals."

He carried the table out and put it in the courtyard. Chickens ran from him, scattering in all directions. Placement was critical. Wherever he put the table, he needed to make sure he was not able to see Alfonso. If the experiment succeeded, the electromagnetic wave would have to penetrate through the hill in front of him. That would be the magic moment. With the care of a parent, he placed the balls for the spark gap, the telegrapher's key, the coherer, the induction coil, and the battery onto the table. A brisk wind blew his hat off, threatening his concentration. He picked it up out of the dust, brushed it off, and jammed it more securely on his head. He would not let anything distract him today.

Neither Alfonso nor Mignani had yet appeared by the time he finished setting up his instruments, so he went to find them.

Alfonso was still in bed, with his wiry hair scarcely visible over his coverlet. Guglielmo pounced on him like a cat and roused him abruptly. Alfonso stumbled into his clothes, sleep wrinkles marking his face.

Guglielmo found Mignani in the lab, his shiny black-suited back already bent over, tightening the screws on the receiver, making sure everything was ship-shape. Guglielmo shivered. Whenever he was truly engaged with something, he tended to run a fever. He took out a handkerchief and wiped the beads of sweat from his brow. Working together, Guglielmo and Mignani carefully carried the receiver downstairs and met Alfonso in the kitchen. Still groggy, he had a rifle in one hand and a slice of Maria's bread in the other.

Guglielmo laid out the plan once more. Alfonso and Mignani would take the receiver and the rifle out to where the willows arched over the stream. Guglielmo had chosen the spot carefully—a place tucked well behind the intervening hill, two and a half kilometers (1.5 miles) away. Alfonso and Mignani would travel up and over the hill, threading their way through the rows of grapes, and disappear over the horizon.

Guglielmo had set a table up under the willows the day before, and Alfonso and Mignani would set the receiver on the table and wait until 8:00 a.m. He made them take out their pocket watches and synchronize them so there could be no mistake. At exactly 8:00 a.m., he would send out an electromagnetic wave. If the receiver picked it up, they would immediately fire the rifle into the air. (He had already tested to see if he could hear it from the barnyard.)

They shook hands all around, recognizing that this moment was a culminating one. Up to now, Guglielmo's experiments had been relatively incremental, but this was a leap. If they were successful, nothing would ever be the same. They would prove that electromagnetic waves could pass through something as thick and immobile as a hill. If all went well, the wave would go through the crisp morning air, the lime-green wine leaves, the pitch-black dirt, the gopher holes, the silent sedimentary rock, and continue through the second layer of dirt, the gopher holes, the vineyard leaves, out into the air again, and meet with the receiver that sat on the table under the willow trees near the stream.

History would be made.

At 7:00 a.m., Alfonso and Mignani set off, looking like they were going out to shoot quail. Alfonso had the rifle slung over his shoulder, his hat at a cocky angle. Mignani carried the receiver, which was covered with a white cloth. Guglielmo watched them go, his heart beating hard, his skin hot to the touch. He hovered over the table, fiddling with the various accoutrements, putting his hand on each like a priest putting his hand on a child's head. The coherer, the battery, the telegraphy key, the transmitter.

He found that he could not sit still, so he paced. This was the life of an inventor, he thought. It was like a play, with its ups and downs, conflicts, failures, and bright successes. He was certain that he was engaged in a race. There were other men out there who were on the same path. They were seeing the same technical and physical patterns. They had the imagination, the guts, the knowledge. He could feel them working in their labs, trying new techniques, imaging new outcomes. He imagined his legs pumping around an oval gravel track, the others gaining, their breath loud as they came up behind him.

Guglielmo took out his watch and looked at the time. The chickens clucked. A dog howled in the distance. A donkey brayed in the barn. He picked up a stick and tapped it rhythmically against the side of the well. Using the tin cup that hung from a hook on the side, he drew some water from the well and had a drink. Time crawled on its hands and knees.

Finally, it was eight o'clock. Guglielmo bent over the coherer and tapped out an "S" in Morse code with his index finger. Dot dot dot. He paused.

He heard a gunshot.

Pigeons flew out of the ash tree.

He almost fell out of his chair.

They had done it. They had succeeded.

Guglielmo could hardly contain the feeling that blossomed from his heart. He knew this morning was like no other morning, and that all mornings after this would be different as well. The world had tilted into a new frame of reference, a new way of thinking, a new way of being. He had drawn a line between before and after.

Guglielmo felt it in every cell of his body. It must have been just like this when fire was discovered, he thought. Or when the wheel was invented. He took a moment to savor this expansive certainty. It was strange, how quickly things had changed. Science could be like that. People would be able to communicate across the world without wires, and signal each other through mountains and over rivers. Somehow, he knew this.

He put his palm to his temple. It had cooled. He gazed toward the hill that had seemed so solid and impenetrable. Even the hill had changed. Now, it seemed more like a net, something you might catch fish in. His waves, like water, could pass straight through, like water through a sieve when you brought up a sparkling bream.

People would know him. They would hear his name and never forget it. His father would be proud of him. Finally, he would understand.

Maria came out of the house carrying a basket of laundry. Guglielmo grabbed her by the waist and swung her around until she lost her grip on the basket and it fell in the dirt. She squawked at him, echoing the chickens around them, but he just grinned and laughed and howled to the heavens "I did it!" He danced her around the yard until she begged for release. He sat her down on the brick wall and danced a jig all on his own.

As Alfonso and Mignani came around the hill, they saw Guglielmo dancing. They ran toward him, and all three danced as though St. Vitus had gotten hold of them. It was true; a madness had its grip on them. But when his mother came into the yard, Guglielmo stopped, suddenly calm. He walked to her, took her hand, and said, "Nothing will ever be the same again." She looked into his dark eyes, so mature for his age, and knew it was true.

Chapter Fourteen

OUT OF ITALY: 1896

Annie, encumbered by a hatbox, hurried along behind Guglielmo. Behind her, Mignani carried a satchel full of food and a portmanteau. Steam suddenly vented out from between the train's wheels, and Annie half-screamed and jumped. When she caught Guglielmo looking back at her, she started laughing. Her laugh sounded like her singing: melodic and fluttering, like a wren. Generally stern, Guglielmo laughed, too. He walked back toward her, took the hatbox, and carried it with one finger. At twenty-one, he was slight but strong.

Annie almost tripped over her voluminous black travel skirt and had to hold on tight to her dark purple hat with its three feathers and its large black bow. But her eyes sparkled as she caught herself. She practically leaped onto the train steps, and he followed behind her, as exuberant as she was.

Tears followed the laughter, and as the train pulled out of the station, they both leaned out the window. Annie fluttered her handkerchief at the faces below. Giuseppe was inscrutable; who knew what was behind that craggy face? Alfonso seemed happy. Perhaps now he could take more time with his girlfriend of the moment, a lively young woman from town who was very proud of her fiery broodmare.

Mignani, visibly upset, kept taking out his handkerchief and blowing his nose. Over the years, he had formed a close bond with Guglielmo. He was a natural scientist and had a certain methodical care that was necessary for the delicate work. Guglielmo had tried to get his father to let him come to London, but on that matter, his father was clear: Mignani was far too valuable at the Villa Griffone and would return to his daily routine of keeping the place running like a Swiss steel pocket watch.

Guglielmo and Annie settled into a private compartment. The green baize wall coverings set off her red hair, which seemed to flash on and off in the sporadic sunlight as the train began to pull out of the station. Guglielmo was reminded of Morse code. He looked at her for a moment with distance, as though she was a stranger. She was still relatively young and had the heartiness of her Irish ancestors. Her round face with its slight sprinkling of freckles was radiant, her smile so wide that it made the skin around her green eyes wrinkle at the corners.

They were finally on their way to London. They would travel by train through Torino, Grenoble, and on to Paris. From Paris, they would continue until they reached the charming sea port of Boulogne-sur-Mer, and they would then take the ferry across the English Channel to Dover. From there it was a quick train trip to London where they would be met by Annie's cousin, Henry Jameson-Davis at Victoria Station. It was all planned.

Part of Guglielmo wished they had not had to resort to going to England. He was already a little homesick for the rolling hills and the dappling, easy sunlight as it filtered through the ash and willow trees. He watched as the scenery, with its stately poplars and warm vineyards, passed by. At times, the scenery disappeared within his mind as he visualized the interior of the little black box he cradled in his arms. He envisioned the coherer, a delicate glass tube, and the slivers of metal filings inside: 95 percent nickel, 5 percent silver. He had spent hundreds of hours finding just the right recipe.

It was like Maria's fine soufflés. Over a lifetime of cooking, she had perfected just the right combination of ingredients. But unlike soufflés, Guglielmo's black box was one of a kind. It was like a painting. It was his work of art.

Guglielmo and Annie had tried to interest the Italian government in his work. They had consulted with the two most important men in the village, the town doctor and the town priest. They had all met in the priest's modest manse, a small gray box attached to the back of the village church. The interior was whitewashed, and it was clear that the priest favored the simplicity of a Spartan lifestyle. Herbs hung drying from the rafters, and a small fire had been laid for the guests. They sat at a rough walnut table and discussed what to do.

Over a plate of cheese and bread and a small carafe of wine, it was decided that they should contact the minister of post and telegraph. Although Guglielmo could imagine many applications for his invention, they all agreed that it ultimately was something that could and should be used for communication.

The minister responded with the usual language. All Guglielmo remembered was the word "regret." It was one more setback. Guglielmo was starting to understand that part of being an inventor was to become as thick-skinned as any painter who suffered multiple rejections. Italy had let him down.

Through relatives and acquaintances, Annie had used her many connections in England to set up a series of meetings, interviews, and presentations. Seated on the train, ignoring the scenery out the window, she pulled out their itinerary and began to pencil notes on the side. This man was notoriously fond of feta cheese, she wrote. This minister knew all there was to know about orchids. This doctor fancied himself a master of whist. Annie knew that the game of getting people to do what you wanted was to show interest in their interests, then woo them with yours. It was a simple strategy that had gotten her invited to the better parties and ultimately landed her a husband.

Guglielmo dozed, his head leaning awkwardly against the window. He let himself be lulled by sound. The rhythm of the steel wheels clicking along the tracks, the murmur of voices, the occasional squeal of a child. It was all comforting. He could even hear the cool, slippery sound of his mother turning the pages of her *La Tribuna Illustrata*. He opened his eyes to slits and glimpsed her, a woman in a red coat lined with fur.

What would happen next? Would he return in a few weeks, looking like a farm dog caught with a chicken hanging from his jaws? Or would he flourish? Would he be able to convince people that he had something worth showing? He worried about a pimple on his cheek that he could feel was ready to erupt. Who would listen to someone barely out of his teens? They would laugh at him. They would snub him. He thought back to his childhood. Those days seemed so far away, as though he was remembering another boy's life. He sighed, and his mother reached over to adjust the coat that had fallen from his shoulders.

He owed her a lot. She was the one who truly believed. She had always been at his side. And she had prepared for this journey like a general plans for his marching army. They would slide into England's technical community on a carpet made of letters of introduction. It had taken six months to arrange. He was grateful to her, but he let his coat slide down again, knowing that it would slightly irritate her. He fell back to sleep, and this time he slept deeply.

Guglielmo felt as though he had slept the entire trip, and he was sleeping again when a train whistle bolted him awake. The sun was just coming up, and they were pulling into London's Victoria Station. Guglielmo's heart was pounding so hard he felt it would burst through his chest. He tried to take deep breaths, but his body was too frightened. He was thinking about the bombings that had taken place in 1880. The Fenians—the Irish Republican Brotherhood—had been behind them, and many people had been injured. Guglielmo opened his eyes and looked up.

Annie was beside him, calmly collecting tin cups and small glass plates and putting them back into the portmanteau. She patted her hair. "I'm a mess," she said, and yawned. She stood up and stretched as far as her dress would let her. For this journey, she had dressed more formally than usual, which meant she was a bit limited in her movements.

They gathered their belongings, Guglielmo taking special care of his instrument box, and disembarked.

He couldn't believe the noise. It was worse than Rome. And the smell was worse, too. Horse manure and soot. And dust. He sneezed three times in quick succession. Welcome to London!

With the help of a porter, they brought all their parcels to the customs shed. Guglielmo insisted on carrying the black box himself. They joined a long line of passengers waiting to get checked through. People carried dogs, parrot cages, even parcels of dirt. By the time Guglielmo and Annie finally got inside the shed, they were exhausted. Even Annie's feathers were limp.

Everything went well until the end, when Guglielmo relinquished his black box. The minute the customs officers opened the box with its mysterious wires and odd-looking apparatus, their attitude changed. The two men visibly bristled, the veins on their foreheads pulsing. World leaders had been in the crosshairs. Even their beloved Queen Victoria had been shot at. They began to pull the delicate objects out of their purple velvet beds, and by the time they were finished examining them, most had been bent, chipped, broken, or crushed.

Guglielmo felt bent, chipped, broken, and crushed. The game was lost before it had begun. He and Annie exited the customs shed, dragging their parcels and the now worthless box. Annie collapsed on a nearby bench and dabbed at her tears before they could fall. Guglielmo sat beside her in stunned silence.

It took them both a moment to realize that someone was talking to them. It was Henry Jameson-Davis, and he had arrived like a gust of energetic wind. Blond, blue-eyed, and dressed in emerald green, he reminded Guglielmo of a leprechaun. Cousin Henry had searched everywhere before spying them on the depot bench, looking crushed and defeated.

Guglielmo opened the box in a mute display. Cousin Henry tutted through his teeth and said, "No worries. We will fix you right up." And he did.

Chapter Fifteen

THE PATENT: 1896

Cousin Henry was well-liked, well-heeled, and well-connected, three qualities that guaranteed access to all the right people. He brought Annie and Guglielmo back to his substantial house in Kensington, where they had hot baths and a good meal.

Cousin Henry's house was comfortable and quiet. After a marvelous meal of shepherd's pie, they were ushered back to their adjoining bedrooms, with high ceilings and chair rails that skirted the expansive rooms.

For Guglielmo, sleep was impossible. Disaster had struck, yet thanks to Cousin Henry, it felt like a minor bump in the road. He stared at the ceiling high above him and ran the day through his mind. It had taken everything he had not to leap upon the custom agents and throttle them until they turned blue. He felt a pain in his stomach. Maybe he was coming down with a cold or the flu. Maybe he had already been destroyed by a trick of fate.

Guglielmo got up and looked through the lace curtains at the city. The moon was almost full and lit the empty street below. Tomorrow the street would be filled with people, carriages, and even a few automobiles, coughing out fumes, making the milk horses rear in terror.

Automobiles, electric lights. He would join this amazing parade of progress. He stretched, cracking his back, and for a moment, he felt confident. He would succeed.

Cousin Henry proved to be not only a good family friend but also a serious supporter of Guglielmo's invention. He introduced him to several friends who were skilled carpenters and machinists. They took one look at the wreckage within Guglielmo's black box and literally rolled up their striped sleeves. They, too, made light of the destruction, telling Guglielmo he would have an entire new apparatus within a week.

The first thing Guglielmo did when he received it was demonstrate it to Henry, who had a habit of wringing his hands when he was excited. He was wringing them when the bell rang. At the sound, he tumbled backwards into his leather desk chair like a tree being felled and exclaimed, "Momentous!"

Henry was a man of imagination, and he immediately understood how important Guglielmo's invention could be. He insisted that Guglielmo begin the process of getting a patent, and he began introducing the invention to people he trusted.

Guglielmo applied himself to the art of patent writing with the same determined focus he had applied to the creation of his invention. His mother and Henry hosted a series of small soirees where they began to talk about this amazing phenomenon.

Annie began to realize that this process was not going to take place in a few weeks. It could take months. Although Cousin Henry had graciously opened his house for their use, it was clear that they needed a place of their own. Soon, much of her time was taken up by finding just the right place.

She knew she was bordering on impropriety by traveling alone, without her husband. When she went to meet prospective landlords, they invariably looked behind her, expecting a husband to make his appearance. It always took time to explain her situation: the brilliance of her favorite son, the reason her husband had not come to London with them (he needed to stay home to run the villa), and the likelihood that she was smart enough to pay the rent on time. Finally, she found a suitable place to rent, and they moved from Cousin Henry's house to new lodgings at 71 Hereford Road.

Henry played cribbage on Saturday nights with a patent lawyer. Henry offered to forgive his cribbage debts if he would help Guglielmo with the patent process. In truth, the patent lawyer, a man with a stomach like a shelf, did not do much of the work. But when Guglielmo brought him a series of drafts, he would look through them, make corrections and edits, and send them back to Guglielmo for more writing. Annie, too, was a capable writer. She worked hard by Guglielmo's side while making sure that he remembered to eat.

To Guglielmo, it felt like he was in his own personal regatta. He could feel the hand of God at his back, gently encouraging here, holding back there, spurring him on like an avid spectator. Guglielmo knew he had to get his patent papers correctly registered before anyone else. Others were out there, working on similar inventions. All were older, wiser, and more experienced than he was. He saw them as his elders, captains of their own yachts, tacking cleverly, taking advantage of each small breeze.

～

It took four months of careful writing, with no shortcuts or loopholes. Finally, one bright afternoon in late May, the process was finished. It was time for Guglielmo to show his invention to the world. He and Annie sat in the study on Hereford Road, where a large desk stood in the middle of the room. A shaft of sunlight lit the neat pile of patent papers. Mother and son sipped tea in silence, understanding their lives were about to change dramatically. They would either succeed or fail. Guglielmo, now twenty-two, took a small bite of a scone, stared at the pile of papers, and shivered a little.

The London Patent Office was housed in a small building between a French dress shop and a shoe store. One could easily miss it. On June 2, 1896, Guglielmo, Henry, and Annie took an open carriage and arrived at the office, just as one of the clerks was propping the door open with an iron Scottish Terrier. They left several pounds lighter. British Patent No. GB12039—"Improvements in Transmitting Electrical Impulses and Signals, and in Apparatus Therefor" by Guglielmo Marconi—had been officially applied for. On July 2, 1897, it would be accepted.

Chapter Sixteen

THE BELL: 1896

Annie adjusted Guglielmo's tie with her strong Irish hands. They were going to meet a man who could make or break their future, and they hoped to stun him with their demonstration. It would be like a magic show. But this magic would not simply be a sleight-of-hand trick that ended after the gaslights had been turned off. Their show would be the beginning of a long and profitable business.

Both Cousin Henry and Annie had been busy during the patent process. They had talked with family and friends about how best to proceed. It was all about finding the right individual, for in this business, as in most affairs, the right person was akin to the right key to a lock. The door would open to a new opportunity.

After many discussions, glasses of sherry, and mugs of beer, Cousin Henry convinced Alan Archibald Campbell-Swinton to visit his home for the purpose of observing a demonstration. Swinton was a young Scottish inventor with a nose like a potato and a moustache like a chimney sweep's brush. He was well respected within the inventor community, and his word of introduction could sweep aside many of the professional obstacles in Guglielmo's path.

When Guglielmo's small brass bell rang, Swinton leaped up and began pacing the drawing room. He understood immediately the importance of what he had seen. "A pen!" he demanded, and then and there he scribbled a letter to the one man who could truly help Guglielmo: William Henry Preece, engineer-in-chief of the British General Post Office.

Preece was a man with the needed sensibilities, interests, and position. He himself was an inventor. If anyone could understand the ramifications of the brass bell ringing, it would be Preece, for he was laced with both imagination and practicality.

Preece was a man who saw a problem and tried to fix it. For example, August 1896 was a terrible month for train disasters. A train going from Charing Cross to Hastings had derailed when it collided with a threshing machine. A Lancaster and Yorkshire Railway passenger train had collided with a West Lancaster Railway passenger train, resulting in one fatality and seven injuries. And a London and North Western Railway sleeping car had derailed at Preston. Fed up, Preece developed several improvements in railway signaling systems. Fewer people were injured, fewer people died.

Preece was also famously interested in telephones. He had brought them into Britain and was instrumental in bringing them to Plymouth for a meeting of the British Association for the Advancement of Science. He had been in attendance when Alexander Graham Bell first demonstrated them to Queen Victoria in 1878 and said she heard some singing quite plainly. She was rumored to have said that the whole process was quite extraordinary.

During the past two years, Preece had become interested in a strange phenomenon involving telegraph wires. Messages delivered by the underground telegraph wires owned by the post office were being picked up by wires above ground owned by a private telegraph company. This seemed impossible. How could the messages be jumping from under the ground to the wires above? It was either providence or science. Preece, who preferred exploring the latter, had tried several experiments, hoping to replicate the phenomena reliably. All were unsuccessful.

On a day in 1896, a carriage stopped in front of Preece's house, known as Gothic Lodge. The home was well-named, with windows shaped like miniature Middle Eastern turrets and double chimneys along the spine of the roof. Annie, Henry, and Guglielmo went through the heavy wooden white gate and knocked on the big oak door. They were let into a foyer with a polished parquet floor and a sweeping staircase.

They met Preece in his den, a place crammed with books, papers, maps, railroad lanterns, a globe, and a stuffed raven. Above the fireplace was a painting of a plump blond woman in a muted blue dress. Preece rose from his chair, a man made of a rusty beard and a firm handshake. Guglielmo liked him immediately.

That day was limited to tea and crumpets, for this was an introductory meeting. Guglielmo could not eat a crumb. But the conversation quickly went from formalities to excitement as Guglielmo described, in his clipped, correct English, where he was in his process, and what he had brought with him to England.

Preece immediately scheduled a time for the demonstration. They would meet the next morning at the General Post Office.

A surprise pre-dawn shower rinsed the morning clean. Raindrops hung from the eaves and the oak trees as the carriage bearing Annie, Cousin Henry, and Guglielmo splashed through the streets. When they pulled up before the imposing edifice of the General Post Office, Guglielmo had a moment of doubt. It was as though the Ionic columns were admonishing him. They were classic Greek architectural icons—sixth century, a style over a thousand years old. For a moment, Guglielmo felt small. His mother, sensing his mood, took his hand for a split second and squeezed it. He carefully picked up two black satchels and entered the building.

The cavernous room was filled with light, sound, and people rushing madly from place to place. The hard walls and pressed tin ceiling did nothing to dim the clattering.

Guglielmo was relieved when they were finally ushered into Preece's small, cluttered office. Preece cleared a table, placing all the papers on the floor, and offered Annie his patent leather desk chair. Guglielmo took his time placing everything exactly where he wanted it. The balls for the spark gap, the telegrapher's key, the coherer, the induction coil, and the battery were on one end of the table, and the bell sat alone on the other end. They were like actors waiting to play their roles. Preece bent over each object in turn, scrutinized them through his gold-rimmed glasses.

Finally, Guglielmo was ready. He pressed the telegrapher's key, and the bell on the other side of the table rang. Preece slowly straightened and stared at Guglielmo. His hand, seemingly of its own volition, waved in front of the bell as though looking for an unseen wire. Then he grabbed Guglielmo's hand and shook it.

It was the beginning of a wonderful friendship.

Guglielmo looked out from behind the red velvet curtain. There was not one empty seat at Toynbee Hall, a large lecture theater in East London. He could see his mother in the front row, resplendent in a yellow sienna dress, fluttering an oriental fan. The place was hot with anticipation.

Preece came out, and the gaslights were lowered. He had a peculiar voice that cracked and splintered when he was excited. When he opened his mouth to introduce Senor Marconi, his voice broke as though he was a schoolboy. He began by describing the state of telegraphy: the limited successes so far, the many attempts, and the possibilities of how life could change if someone conquered this technological problem. He then introduced Guglielmo.

Although Guglielmo had been nervous while listening to Preece's introduction, the minute he went on stage, the nervousness ceased. Perhaps it was because his equipment was waiting for him there. He had spent most of the early part of the evening polishing the wood, the glass, the metal. Everything gleamed. Everything was pristine.

The *Daily Chronicle* later reported, "The apparatus was then exhibited. What appeared to be just two ordinary boxes were stationed at each end of the room, the current was set in motion at one end and a bell was immediately rung in the other. To show there was no deception, Mr. Marconi held the receiver and carried it about, the bell ringing whenever the vibrations at the other box were set up."

The impact on the crowd was immediate. They bolted to their feet and began clapping and shouting. They even rushed the stage. Had it not been for the nimble assistants standing ready, several members of the audience would have stormed the delicate equipment and perhaps broken it.

Most people in the audience were inventors in their own rights. Creators of steamships, telephones, diesel engines, and medicinal patents, they were united in being able to see into the future. They knew they lived in an age of furious innovation: scientific feats building on the discoveries of others, new materials generating new ideas.

Because Preece was so trusted and well respected, Guglielmo was immediately trusted as well. A few Americans clapped him on the back. The English wanted to shake his hand. The few women there wanted his autograph.

Guglielmo went home that night and, as was his custom, retired early and lay in bed with his hands behind his head, reviewing the past few weeks. He and Preece had set up his equipment in several circumstances, and each time, it had worked like a Swiss clock. They had stayed up late, spinning stories of what one could do with this new technology. They could use it to save the lives of sailors. They could help communicate with trains. One night, after quite a few glasses of wine, they discussed Jules Verne's science fiction novel *Off on a Comet* and speculated that Guglielmo's invention could have allowed the people carried away by the comet to communicate with their families on the Earth far below.

Guglielmo was in heaven. At last, he had a friend he could talk to. Someone else who could imagine the unimaginable.

Chapter Seventeen

THE BUNGALOW AT STONEHENGE:
LA CALMA DELLA MIA VITA EBBE ALLORA FINE
(THE CALM OF MY LIFE ENDED THEN): 1897

Guglielmo stood on Easton Hill. Beneath him was the Salisbury Plain, a chalk plateau with a few beech trees and a smattering of small villages. It was perfect for a long-range demonstration of his little black box.

The day before, he had visited Stonehenge. As he wandered between the ancient pillars, he had felt the hands of history. If all went well, perhaps he could be a historical pillar of some kind. He shoved the thought away as frivolous and started down the hill toward the four men who waited for him.

They had found a small wooden shack they fondly called the Bungalow. It held a small stove for preparing afternoon tea, a table for making repairs and holding the sending device, and four thick, squat chairs ideal for resting in after a long tromp across the plains.

Once inside, Guglielmo paid attention to one man, George Kemp. This British Post Office engineer, with this handlebar moustache and his red hair parted neatly in the middle, had eyes that gleamed with intelligence, thoroughness, and a kind of workingman's peace. Guglielmo had always respected people whose intelligence flowed not only through their minds but also through their hands, and he watched as Kemp capably and gently handled his equipment.

The respect was mutual. Kemp, like the other workers involved in these experiments, called him Mr. Marconi, even though Guglielmo was half his age. Guglielmo quite liked it when people referred to him as Marconi.

Working together, they continually increased the distance between the sending unit, which had been installed inside the Bungalow, and the receiving unit, which they had installed on a wooden cart so they could move it easily. At first, they were conservative, trying just 100 yards, but they soon pushed the cart to a mile, then 6 miles, and finally 9 miles. When the bell rang at 9 miles, the five men cheered.

The sound startled the rock doves nesting in a nearby stand of juniper, and they scattered into the late afternoon sky. The men started chanting, "Marconi! Marconi!" At that moment, Guglielmo left his boyhood name behind and became Marconi, even to himself.

The news swept England, but responses varied. At least one reporter was openly suspicious and unbelieving. "It may be another Italian with his barrel-organ," one reporter wrote, "but without the monkey, and the organ doesn't play, though it seems to be making noise all the same." Women wrote to Marconi complaining slyly of vibrations under their bare feet. They claimed that these titillating feelings must, of course, be due to his electrical experiments.

Marconi was not immune to these veiled offers of female companionship. He stored the letters in a walnut box and did his best to ignore them. He recognized that women had the capacity to shift his focus. Intellectually and practically, he was like an arrow, on a straight and direct path. He would allow few things into his life that would change his course.

Eventually, the Italian press got wind that one of their own was doing something interesting. *La Tribuna* sent Olindo Malagodi, its London correspondent, to interview him in depth. For the first time, Marconi was asked about the technical end of his experiments. He responded in detail, telling Malagodi all about that amazing day when his waves had succeeded in penetrating the hills behind his house. He ended the account by saying, "The idea of telegraph communication by these means and without metal wires came to me in the summer of 1895."

Unlike many inventors, Marconi already had a steely focus on business. Perhaps it was the influence of his father, but even as early as 1897, a business plan was forming in his head. By citing 1895 as the year of his idea, he was positioning himself in time ahead of other inventors. His own voice, speaking through the newspaper, would come in handy if anyone ever challenged who had thought of it first.

Marconi now embarked on a series of semi-public experiments. He demonstrated his apparatus on rooftops, in theaters, and in the drawing rooms of the rich. He was flying high on a whirlwind of successes, and the international press began to pay attention to this slim young Italian.

Even the Italians showed more interest. Almost a year after Marconi had left for England, he was sent back home because Annibale Ferrero, Italy's ambassador in London, had noticed that the British Royal Navy was taking an interest in Marconi and his invention. It was as though Marconi was standing in a flock of turkeys, and one by one, their heads were popping up.

If Marconi had held his first demonstrations in Rome at the Palazzo Sant'Agostino, the home of the Italian Navy, he would have been extremely nervous. Outside, it was an imposing rectangular four-story building with a clock tower on one end. Inside, it was all gilt ceilings and red velvet, gold braids of silk rope and chandeliers.

As Marconi and Kemp set up his apparatus on a small wooden stage at one end of a large room filled with chairs, people began arriving. They looked remarkably like their environs: loops of braid, shiny medals, red trim. These men were the cream of the naval and political crop. Senators, generals, admirals, and businessmen crowded in. Their voices rumbled through the cigar smoke, and Marconi could sense their excitement.

Of all the possible applications for Marconi's invention that were bandied about, none was more compelling than using it at sea. The loneliness and vulnerability of sailors at sea was a constant problem. Communications, whether about military positions or the birth of a baby, had to wait until a ship was close to shore. Marconi's invention could change everything, and these powerful men were starting to realize that.

Marconi and Kemp were about to begin the demonstration when they realized they had forgotten to bring two poles that would elevate the aerials that they now used. Assistants and secretaries were dispatched in search of the proper poles, but none could be found. Marconi was in a panic. He had finally gotten the attention of his country, and he would be defeated by the lack of two sticks! He charged out into the hallway and spied a bucket, a mop, and a broom. He grabbed the mop and broom and was able to conduct the demonstration.

Once more, Marconi's innate inventiveness had saved him. He almost felt like a boy again, experimenting with objects he had scraped together. As he made the bell ring, the men huddled in groups, already scheming on how the invention could be used.

The news traveled fast. Not long after, Marconi was in his hotel room, having a breakfast of shirred eggs, when he received a letter with the seal of the king and queen of Italy. They were inviting him for an audience. Marconi almost choked on his hot chocolate.

The Palazzo Sant'Agostino had not prepared him for the opulence of the Palazzo del Quirinale, the sixth largest palace in the world. As he was led through the rooms, he couldn't help but compare it to home. Villa Griffone was a comfortable three-story building, large enough to house a family of ten. Here was a home that could have housed a thousand, or so it seemed to him at the time.

Each room was grander than the next. Floor-to-ceiling tapestries depicting ancient hunts, oval paintings of creamy-skinned ancestors, flocked red-and-gold wallpaper, and ornate ceilings that stretched two stories all made Marconi feel small.

At last, he was conducted into a room with tall curtained windows and plush white satin chairs. Queen Margherita and King Umberto were seated on thrones that arched up behind them. She wore a pale rose gown and long strands of pearls; he was dressed formally, with a red sash and loops of silken rope.

Both plied Marconi with questions, asking how he had managed to create such a marvelous thing, where he had gotten his ideas, and what uses he thought his invention would be best suited for. When King Umberto got especially enthusiastic about an idea, he tugged on his bushy moustache. The queen fingered the pearls around her neck when Marconi painted a picture of life at Villa Griffone. She sighed, as if she longed for a different time. Marconi briefly imagined her as a child, wandering through the fields near his house. He could see her there quite easily.

Finally, the royal couple rose, the king clicked his heels, and Marconi was ushered out as quickly as he had been ushered in. As the gilded wood door closed noiselessly behind him, he breathed deeply, then realized he had not done that since he arrived.

Marconi sat in his room at the Quirinale Hotel, reading letters from his parents. They were thrilled that he had been to see the king and queen. His mother had always been enamored of royalty, and Marconi knew she would take great pleasure in picturing them talking earnestly with her son. She inquired about his clothing, his health, and whether he had brought the proper shoes.

His father, on the other hand, was all business. He was quite insistent that his new company bear the Marconi name. That left Marconi with a sour taste in his mouth. Did his father want that for him or for himself? He couldn't quite decide, then realized it scarcely mattered. It was good advice.

Marconi thought about his father, and how he had changed. When Marconi was a child, Giuseppe had seemed aloof, interested in his son only when he made some terrible gaffe. Then his fiery temper would emerge, subsiding when punishment had been bestowed. Now, however, he was dealing with him respectfully, man to man. Marconi wondered if it had to do with money. His invention had captured the minds of businessmen in England and Italy, something of which his father finally approved.

Marconi went back home to Villa Griffone the next week. It was strange to visit after so much had transpired. As soon as he walked through the door, his mother smothered him with kisses. Marconi did his best not to wriggle away too quickly. Maria plied him with his favorite foods; *braciole, osso buco, bigoli*. This, he had missed.

He found it small. His bed, the rooms, the shed behind the house; all had shrunk while he was away. Countless times, he measured his height. He wandered the open fields and visited the site of his now defunct still. The willows closed in on him, and the paths were mere threads. He left in a hurry, anxious to get back to the house.

He fell into his childhood bed, exhausted. The wind, the rain, and the constant stress of managing his team, his materials, and his possible donors had taken their toll. The minute his head hit the pillow, he was out.

The next day, he sat down with his father in his den, remembering the years of harsh treatment. Had there really been a time when he was terrified of this stooped old man? When his father offered him a sherry, Marconi took it and thanked him. He listened to his father's counsel, nodding in agreement. He would return to London and start his company.

Chapter Eighteen

Marconi lowered his binoculars and wiped rain out of his eyes. The tugboat *Flying Huntress* was out there somewhere, but the clouds and the rain obscured his vision. Nature was both his friend and his enemy. It had been consistently stormy, with high winds and heavy seas. On the one hand, this made everything almost unbearably difficult, with the men on board constantly seasick, and the cold deep enough to drill into your bones. On the other, it was a real trial. If the tests worked, they would know the apparatus could tolerate barometric shifts and heavy rains, as well as penetrate through land.

He returned to the hotel, where George Kemp offered him a mug of hot chocolate. Marconi sat in the private sitting room and let the mug warm his chilled fingers. He imagined a ship driven upon the rocks, pummeled by 30-foot waves. He pictured an operator frantically sending Morse code through a Marconi radio set. He envisioned a receiver on land and a solitary man sitting before it in a shack, receiving the message and sending it on to the British Coastguard. He saw men roused from their beds, hastily pulling on their pants, leaping to their rescue boats and casting off. He saw them as they rounded the coast and began pulling the survivors from the wreck. Marconi sipped, smiled, and said to Kemp, "Let's try sending the message again."

Marconi had chosen the Isle of Wight for good reasons. It was relatively close to London, yet rugged enough to be free of most people. He had settled into the Royal Needles Hotel in Alum Bay. The hotel staff had allowed him to take over the sitting room and drill a small hole in the window pane. He had strung the cable from the sending apparatus through the window and up onto the flagpole.

On a clear day, one could sit in the deck chairs on the front lawn and see the white rocky "needles" the hotel was named for, spires of cliffs that ran out to sea like a line of sharks' teeth. Not that Marconi spent much time sitting. Most of his time was spent in endless trials, trying to increase the distance or the clarity of the message. The receiving aerial on the tug was now 18 meters high. The Americans would call it 59 feet, although why they insisted on using their feet as measuring devices was beyond Marconi's understanding.

In an attempt to create ever higher receiving aerials, Marconi had looked back to his childhood and the kites he had built and sent high in the air around the Villa Griffone. Since arriving on the Isle of Wight, he had successfully launched kites several times and used them to receive signals from the sending station. Unfortunately, kites could not withstand harsh weather.

But Marconi was tenacious, like his childhood bulldog, Bella. He would try and try again. He finished his chocolate and grabbed up his binoculars, ready to send yet another message to the tug. They would build a taller antenna on shore and begin sailing the tug around the bay, testing and retesting its limits.

Chapter Nineteen

THE REGATTA AND THE QUEEN: 1898

Marconi woke early and stretched. He jumped into his clothes, eager to get onto the deck of the *Flying Huntress*. The sea smelled faintly of pickles. It must be the brine, he thought in some small part of his mind, but the rest was taken up with the task ahead: covering the Kingston Regatta in Dublin Bay for two newspapers, the *Daily Express* and the *Evening Mail*, by wireless. He was now a kind of reporter! The thought made him smile. This was a role he had not imagined himself playing.

Marconi had never been in Ireland before. He found it as green and grand as he had imagined when, as a child, he had read a book about the pot of gold at the end of the rainbow. He remembered reading it for the first time. It was on one of his sails with Daisy, his cousin. He thought back on those transcendent sailing days and breathed in deeply. The sea would always be in his blood.

In the dining room, he met Kemp, who was enjoying a breakfast of scrambled eggs, toast, coffee, orange juice, pancakes, sausage, and bacon. Kemp laughed when Marconi sat down and ordered toast and an espresso. "That would keep me going for five minutes," Kemp said between bites. He had already checked and double-checked the transmitter, making sure it was ready for the races. Earlier, they had installed a receiver at a newspaper office in Kingston, and it was ready to receive messages.

The day was a heady one for Marconi. His invention worked perfectly, and a stiff, steady breeze ensured that none of the sailing yachts suffered from the doldrums. Although the boats were ostensibly the stars of the day, the journalists couldn't help but be curious about this slim young man with the dark hair and blue eyes, who so capably and calmly ran his mysterious collection of odd-looking instruments.

Because of Marconi's invention, the newspapers could report on the progress of the yachts even before they could be seen by the crowds on shore. It seemed truly miraculous, and afterwards, Marconi was inundated with interview requests. Among the more interesting were those from the Italian, English, and American navies.

But it was a telegram from Queen Victoria that furthered his goal of eventually sending a message across the Atlantic. The Prince of Wales had twisted his knee while on board the Royal Yacht *Osborne*. The Queen was at her summer residence, Osborne House, and she "wanted the two Osbornes to be able to communicate properly."

It was relatively easily done. First, Marconi fastened a conductor to the mast of the *Osborne* that stretched to a height of 83 feet above deck. Next, he needed to set up a conductor at Osborne House.

The gardens at Queen Victoria's Ladywood Cottage on the grounds of Osborne House smelled of honeysuckle and roses. Wrens sang in the thickets. But Marconi's mind was elsewhere. He was thinking about the fact that Prince Albert's yacht often took cruises along the shoreline. What would happen to the connection then?

Marconi was walking the gardens when he was accosted by a belligerent gardener. He had blond hair and rusty eyebrows and was built like a Viking. He barked at Marconi, asking him what he was doing on the queen's property, and told him in no uncertain terms to go back and around, for the queen was out walking in her bath chair, a type of small carriage drawn by a pony.

Marconi was not used to being shouted at. He looked the hefty gardener up and down and remarked in an icy tone that he would go through the garden or leave. The gardener gestured grandly, pointing the way to the public road.

Marconi bowed stiffly and returned to his hotel. When the queen later learned of this exchange, she told the messenger to "get a new electrician." The messenger replied, "Alas, Your Majesty, England has no Marconi." Marconi got the job.

For sixteen days, Marconi sent daily messages between the queen and her son. Most of the time, it seemed that the prince, limping around the deck, would much rather have been out of communication with his sometimes domineering mother. This was a sentiment Marconi could relate to. Although he loved his mother and she had done much to smooth his way, he was beginning to feel the need to stretch his wings on his own.

The prince and Marconi parted as friends. One of the prince's final words to Marconi was "Mothers!" He gave him a pin as a keepsake.

Chapter Twenty

IT'S A NEW WORLD IN THE NEW WORLD: AMERICA, 1899

The potted palms in the lobby of the Hoffman House Hotel in Manhattan crashed to the marbled floors, and dirt spilled out along the normally pristine lobby. A crystal chandelier came loose on one side and swung crazily until finally stopping, hanging at a dizzying angle.

One of the guests, a thin young man in a yellow-checked suit, was gasping, almost crying as he nervously picked at the upholstery of his chair. The concierge, smelling salts in hand, hastened to inform him that the electrical apparatus Mr. Marconi had brought into the hotel had nothing whatsoever to do with the sudden, alarming events. It had been a boiler explosion.

Marconi's crew attempted to reassure the man by explaining the reason that boilers exploded. Sometimes it was due to the pressure points in a badly seamed boiler, sometimes a safety valve. In a vain attempt to calm the stuttering fellow, they began opening their trunks, and in doing so, discovered that one of the critical trunks was missing.

This was how Marconi's first trip to the United States began. It was a scene of technical tragedy and irrational fear. He heard about it later in the day, after having tea with Thomas Edison.

Edison talked nonstop about himself. Marconi stirred his tea and stared at an attractive woman who sat at the table next to them. Wearing a striped hat with three peacock feathers, she was reading Proust. He thought her eyes were the most beautiful green color. Marconi only half-heard Edison describe how he had saved a three-year-old named Jimmie Mackenzie from a runaway train, how everyone in downtown New York City could now see at night as well as they could during the day, and how he had single-handedly invented the phonograph. But he snapped back to attention when Edison changed the topic.

"Marconi, one of the most amazing things that people never realize is that this air, this very air around us, is filled with all sorts of information," Edison was saying. "This information is just waiting to be plucked out of the air and magnified until we can all hear it."

Marconi stood and explained that his men were waiting for him back at the hotel. On the outside, he appeared bored, but on the inside, he was on fire. This short speech had lit him up as surely as any match would light a crumpled hundred-year-old document.

When Marconi arrived at the Hoffmann House, the scene reminded him of a train derailment. Nothing was at right angles, and everything was out of place. There were no injuries, but people had collapsed in heaps into the lobby chairs. Excited high-pitched voices floated over the general roar. People were demanding their money back and demanding attention. Some were insisting that "this Marconi fellow" be held accountable.

Marconi waded into the fray. Within minutes, he had calmed the man in the checked suit, charmed an elderly woman almost strangling a Pekingese, and sat down with his own men to get a clearer picture of what had happened.

The missing trunk was his biggest worry. One of the most vexing problems he constantly faced was keeping track of the large amount of equipment he needed to transport. Invariably, things went missing. This trunk was one of the most valuable things he possessed. It contained the delicate instruments he relied on for his demonstrations.

He sent two men back to the docks to retrace their steps, two men to check in with the carriage service they had used, two men to search the hotel lobby and the streets outside and the grounds, and two men to the rooms they had rented upstairs. Within an hour, the trunk was found, sitting unseen behind a lobby couch.

Marconi had heard about Delmonico's, and the legendary steak house did not disappoint. Mahogany walls, gilt chandeliers, classic oil portraits, harp-backed chairs, and geometric Indian kilims combined to create an atmosphere of opulence and wealth. He was waiting to dine with James Gordon Bennett Jr., the publisher of the *New York Herald*.

When Bennett entered the room, all the ladies' hats, with their multiple feathers, turned toward him. Marconi briefly thought of a flock of peahens noticing the brightest peacock. Bennett strode up with an American steamship thrust and led with his hand, waiting for a handshake. When Marconi took it, he felt as though his own hand was being pressed into a book.

Not only did Bennett publish news; he made news. He had notoriously sent Henry M. Stanley to find David Livingstone, the Scottish missionary swallowed up by the "Dark Continent."

He was a fan of new technologies and had covered Edison's lighting of central New York and the development of the telegraph.

Marconi and Bennett talked until two in the morning. Marconi felt he had a new friend who understood the relationship between invention, communication, transportation, and patent law. Not only that, Bennett loved to sail.

The reason Marconi had come to the United States in the first place was because Bennett had asked him to cover the upcoming America's Cup that pitched the New York Yacht Club's *Columbia* against the Royal Ulster Yacht Club's *Shamrock*. At first, Marconi had refused, thinking it would be a waste of time. But Marconi's own love of sailing, and the idea that he could turn the experience into a media opportunity, changed his mind. After meeting Bennett, he knew he had chosen correctly.

Theirs would be a symbiotic relationship. Marconi could install 250-foot masts on the SS *Ponce*, a steamship designated for covering the race. If all went to plan, the masts would relay signals via their new Marconi system to a station nearest the coast, and those signals in turn would be relayed by wire to the office of the *New York Herald*.

Everything went to plan and then some. Marconi installed his system and then himself on the SS *Ponce*. Sleek for a steamship, the *Ponce* was defined by a black central smokestack sporting rings of yellow and white. One mast was astern and another was in the bow, which was perfect for Marconi's needs.

Marconi was never one to miss an opportunity to do something first, and he utilized the *Ponce* even before race day. All of New York was waiting for the arrival of Admiral George Dewey, a war hero fresh from the Spanish-American War. Marconi sent the first US ship-to-shore message from an officer on board the *Ponce* to the shore, announcing Dewey's arrival. The city exploded with joy and welcomed the admiral with a two-day ticker tape parade. Unknown to Marconi, a navy man stood among the crowds of cheering people who lined the shore, writing in a small black book.

Race day dawned brilliant and crisp, hinting at the coming of winter. Marconi was prepared with a blue wool pea coat, and he buttoned the flap when he went topside.

Last night had been a brilliant evening on board. The ship's dining room had shone with the human lights of New York City: bankers, reporters, sailors, actors, and best of all, sparkling women. Marconi had been sandwiched between a bearded banker, reputedly worth half of New York, and an actress who was currently lighting up the stage as Roxanne in a musical based on the story of Cyrano de Bergerac. He spent most of the night drinking in the distilled lights of her blue eyes.

Now, however, he began the day. The guns went off and the race was on. Soon Marconi, at his own private helm, was hard at work, sending the messages written by the *Herald* reporters. Throughout the entire day, he and his men sent messages to the *Herald*, giving them on-the-spot, in-the-moment coverage. After the final race was run, he went out to the bow and took a deep breath. The salt air was like a tonic to him. It cooled his lungs and opened his throat.

A man he had not seen before appeared on his port side. He introduced himself as Edward Francis Qualtrough, lieutenant commander of the US Navy. Qualtrough was an enthusiastic if somewhat corpulent man with a sweeping handlebar moustache. He shook Marconi's hand three times, moving it up and down, reminding Marconi of the pump in the backyard of Villa

Griffone. Qualtrough was sure that if Marconi had been in the Philippines, the US Navy would have had an easier time of it. He became one of Marconi's biggest supporters.

The next few months were filled with yet more tests and more dinners with luminaries such as the director of the Metropolitan Museum of Art, the director of the newly established National Commercial Bank of New York, and the director of the Italian Chamber of Commerce. Eventually, Marconi had enough of directors. Every waking hour had been filled with something to do, someone to visit, or someone who wanted to visit him. He had set up a US branch of his company in New York, seen his name in the paper thirty times, and taken part in an American regatta. It was time to go back to England.

Chapter Twenty-One

IN LOVE ON BOARD: JOSEPHINE, 1899

She was dressed in emerald green with small sapphires that dangled and bobbed from her ears. He saw how delicately she cut her filet mignon, and heard the swish of her gown as she stood up. Marconi, who had always appreciated beautiful women, now saw one that made him quiver.

Her name was Josephine Bowen Holman. She was the darling of Indianapolis and had been raised in a family of judges, publishers, and politicians. Educated at Bryn Mawr, she had ideas befitting the modern woman facing a new century. She was as smart as she was beautiful, and Marconi felt he had never seen such a perfect creature. She even knew Morse code.

From Josephine's perspective, Marconi was a slim, athletic, energetic Italian man who spoke English like a Brit, looked her directly in the eye, and respected her opinion. Best of all, he listened. After being introduced by a journalist friend, they became inseparable. They walked the decks from morning to night in all kinds of weather. Sometimes her skirts were wet with fog, sometimes they were hot to the touch from the searing midafternoon heat. By the time they arrived in England, they were completely smitten with each other.

~

Marconi was sweating under his collar. He slipped his index finger under it and pulled it away from his skin. Today, Josephine would meet his mother. He had no idea how that would go.

Josephine, who sat in the carriage next to him, was dressed in a gold satin dress with black piping. She was uncharacteristically quiet, and he realized that she, too, was nervous. She wore short white gloves and carried a small beaded reticule.

They pulled up to his mother's house, got out of the carriage and knocked on the dark green door. Annie opened the door herself. He could see that she was doing her best not to scan Josephine up and down. He saw her stare for a moment into Josephine's eyes. Then she abruptly turned and led them to the parlor.

At first, Marconi couldn't bear it. The two women he was closest to, in the same room, on the same settee, almost touching. The sweat now trickled down his back. His mother was gracious but stiff, smiling like a wooden doll. Josephine had the ease of an American. She complimented Annie on her dress, spoke easily about the roses sitting in a white vase on the piano, and started telling Annie about the book she was currently reading, Robert Louis Stevenson's *The Wrong Box*. She was tempted to talk about the book she was truly fascinated in, Alfred Russell Wallace's *Darwinism: An Exposition of the Theory of Natural Selection with Some of Its Applications*, but she didn't want to appear to be a show-off or, worse, an egghead. That would have been very bad form.

She had chosen well. Annie, too, had read the Stevenson novel, and the two women spent some time parsing the book. By the time they finished wondering about the roots of the word "tontine," they were friends.

Marconi and Josephine had agreed to make all the introductions on one day, so Marconi took Josephine back to her hotel, where they met Josephine's mother and her two sisters for tea. That did not go well. Marconi found Josephine's mother too brash, too fat, too much like one of those chickens that scuttled in the dirt outside of Villa Griffone. Somehow, Josephine's mother had gotten it into her mind that Marconi was only interested in Josephine for her money. True, there were rumors of money trouble within the company, but Marconi thought he had managed to contain most of them.

The tea ended in a kind of social truce. Josephine's mother shook Marconi's hand limply when they left. As far as Marconi was concerned, she was a problem that did not need to be fixed now. He had other, more pressing concerns that needed his attention.

One in particular was "The Great Thing." This "thing" had become Marconi's Holy Grail. He believed that if he could send a message across the Atlantic Ocean via wireless telegraphy, his troubles would dissipate. His money issues, political challenges, and patent insecurities would melt away like snowflakes on a tongue.

As far as he was concerned, this problem could be distilled into three major areas: interference, privacy, and distance. He approached them methodically, like a series of boyhood puzzles. His latest innovation was something he called "tuned circuits." This invention allowed him to tune both his receivers and his transmitters to the same frequency. This new idea would allow him to kill two birds with one stone. Not only could messages become private, they could also help with the interference issue.

Meanwhile, the world was waiting to take its first step into the twentieth century. For pessimists, the world would continue to decay, with the rich getting richer and the poor getting poorer. For optimists, it was a time of change. They believed that technology would fundamentally change human nature, and as dawn broke over the year 1900, people would break out of their eggshells of inhumanity and become a better species.

Josephine had gone back to New York with her family, and she wrote to Marconi almost daily. Marconi wrote back, making sure his letters were free of romance and focused on the business of love, as though love was a laundry list. This was in case they were ever read by the matron of the household.

One night, Marconi stayed out late, dining with his board members after agreeing on his company's new name: Marconi's Wireless Telegraph Company. It had been a long struggle. His father had been especially vocal about insisting that the family name be included in the company name. As Marconi fingered the filigree on the handle of his silver fork, he briefly pondered his father's motivation. Was it simply because he wanted the name of Marconi to be synonymous with the burgeoning fame of the company? Or was it, as his father stated, a way to always maintain control?

Returning home, Marconi spied the latest letter from Josephine. His heart gave a little thump as he tore it open with a letter opener. He was overwhelmed. It was poetic, articulate, and filled with loving warmth. She wrote brilliantly about the importance and rarity of a century passing, likening it to a rare bird seen only once in three generations. She was conscious of the times in which they lived, which were so rich with possibilities, yet so filled with the potential for horror and hate. She had an amazingly perceptive and active mind.

Marconi finished reading the letter and held it to his breast for a moment. Josephine truly was a wonderful girl. Smart, funny, and so beautiful, with her chestnut hair pulled up in a wave away from her forehead.

When he finally went to bed that night, her letter sat on his bedside table. Although he spent the last hour poring over problems at the new sending station at Poldhu in the south of England, the letter was the last thing he looked at before closing his eyes.

Marconi took an extra minute to finish his poached egg. He tried cracking his neck. Recently, he had experienced an occasional shortness of breath. He was sure it was nothing. Simply the body's response to pressure. And he could feel pressures from all sides. Sometimes, during weak and vulnerable times, he felt as though his heart would implode. Nothing was easy.

Nikola Tesla, a cranky, eccentric man, had become a competitive problem. Ironically, Marconi saw himself in the Serbian inventor. Tesla, like Marconi, knew the benefits of being a showman, and in many ways, he had outdone Marconi in his theatricals. As early as 1889, Tesla had opened a lab in New York and dazzled his friends and a variety of artists with entertainments featuring electrical lightning storms that arced madly throughout the space.

There was an ugly rumor that Edison had offered Tesla $50,000 to improve Edison's general setup—his motors and generators. After Tesla accomplished this, Edison laughed, slapped him on the back, and said, "Tesla, you don't understand American humor! I was only joking!" Tesla stared at him for a solid minute, probably contemplating murder, and left Edison's employment without another word.

Now Tesla was threatening Marconi's business by claiming he had a 100-foot-high spark that could jump the Atlantic Ocean as though it was a puddle.

Even if Tesla was grandstanding, Marconi could not afford having anyone else solve his "Great Thing" before he did. He had too much at stake: eight stations in the British Isles; receiving sets on thirty-two ships; stations in France, Belgium, Corsica, and Germany; several portable receiving stations on luxury liners; and some experimental installations in the Italian Navy. So much pressure!

He took another sip of coffee and thought about Josephine. It was June, and a breeze the temperature of her skin floated through the window. Perhaps it was her last letter that had warmed him so. She had been reading about him in the *Herald*—his "numerous and stupendous exploits" and his "world-conquering stations"—and urged him to take care of his health. She expressed her belief that his ideas would change the world forever. She urged him to "eat a strawberry for me, at least one a week." He smiled at that.

She would be an ideal helpmate, one who understood the responsibilities and pressures of his work. Marconi thought of the last time he had seen her in person. It was during his most recent trip to New York, when he was scouting locations for another station. He had squeezed in a half-hour visit, during which Josephine's mother had sat in a pink chair, staring at him through her pince-nez. Josephine had been all smiles, but he had sensed tension in her slim hands as she tried to pour the tea.

That personal visit had been somewhat strained, but the overall business part of the visit had reaped vast rewards.

He had spent weeks scouting the coastline for the perfect spot to begin putting his "Great Thing" in motion. Some of the spots were too far from major roads; some had no access to water; some were too far from the sea. Finally, he had met up with a man called Cook who owned property that, though desolate, had the other needed qualities. It was in South Wellfleet, part of a place called Cape Cod.

Marconi had taken the train as far as possible, then climbed onto Cook's rough farm cart, which smelled of barley. Cook had gestured grandly to the windswept promontory and exclaimed "Voilà!" The deal was sealed with Cook's signature, a big X. Although Marconi told only a few coworkers and, of course, Josephine, he was now positioned to begin trying to conquer the Atlantic.

He was counting on sending a message from Poldhu and receiving it in Cape Cod, but nature had other plans. On September 17, 1901, a serious storm attacked the towers at Poldhu. The 2,200-foot masts that stood over the rocky cove fell like a band of brothers, for they were all bound together with guy wires. When they went down, some of Marconi's men likened the sound to the shrieks and cries of women.

When Marconi received the telegram about the towers, he started drawing on the back of his napkin, for he was at his favorite restaurant, the Criterion. He would reduce the complexity of the station. Two masts, each 160 feet high, would have to do. Otherwise, the project would be set back by at least six months, time Marconi felt he could scarcely afford. Because of the reduction in height, he would need to build a station in the New World that was as close as possible to the one in the Old World.

Chapter Twenty-Two

THE THREE DOTS: 1901

Obstacles come in the form of wind, rain, and stressed metal, but they also come in the form of people and their documents. Before Marconi even had a chance to rebuild and do some serious experimental signaling from Cape Cod, he was told in no uncertain terms to cease and desist by the Anglo-American Telegraph Company, which had an ironclad monopoly on telegraphic communications (even though theirs were by wire).

Marconi, usually adroit at wiggling out of these kinds of requests, decided to move the entire station further north. The Canadians were being very helpful and knew that he adored roast beef with mashed potatoes.

Marconi stumbled into his room at the Cochrane House, a small inn located in St John's, Newfoundland. He was due to meet with Canadian officials in an hour. There was a moment when he wondered if he could. He was flush with fever, and his lungs felt as though they needed more air. He looked at the bed for a moment and imagined lying down. Then he splashed water on his face, combed his hair, and changed into a new suit.

The meeting was miraculously short. The Canadians gave him carte blanche to set up a station at an abandoned diphtheria hospital. His main man, George Kemp, had scoped out the site and declared it perfect. Marconi would see for himself in the morning. He was in bed before ten o'clock and for once slept the entire night.

The morning was a classic Canadian blustery gray winter day. Marconi was driven up to Signal Hill in a horse-drawn cart. Kemp was right; the place was perfect. The cliffs fell straight down to the ocean, and the medical building would house up to twenty men.

Kemp and the rest of Marconi's men were already hard at it by the time he arrived. They were preparing to launch a large white kite. Marconi thought back to that boyhood day when he had flown his first kite. Almost everything was different—the weather, the environs, and the kite itself—but the core idea was the same: use nature to gain altitude.

A single copper aerial wire was attached, and the kite was launched. It savagely grabbed the wind and soared rapidly to 500 feet. It was December 12, 1901. The men were thinking about Christmas. They talked about Christmas pudding, French peas, cranberry jelly, English drawn butter, and roast goose.

Marconi imagined for a moment what he would see from the perspective of the kite. Ragged white lines of pounding surf, a carpet of rough gray water, and upturned faces as they all gazed toward the sky, calculating the kite's strength and capacity.

Marconi was standing near the receiver, as always, listening for a signal that would defeat distance, a signal all the way from Poldhu, from all the way across the Atlantic Ocean.

The physical scientists said it couldn't be done; that a signal, a Hertzian wave, would just charge forever straight out and be lost in the heavens. But Marconi disagreed. He thought that it would curve somehow along the lines of the earth. He had bet his money, time, and effort on that idea.

He listened intently. The wind kept howling around a drain pipe nearby, but suddenly, miraculously, he heard a sharp click as the tapper struck the coherer. A signal was coming. The he heard it. Three little clicks.

Marconi imagined the man who sent them, 2,000 miles away. He would be bent over his apparatus, intent on tapping out the signal for the millionth time. Perhaps he wore glasses and a plaid cap. Perhaps there was a mug of English Breakfast tea at his elbow, gone cold long ago. How could he know that the signal had gone through? That the world had suddenly become smaller?

Distances can be measured in many ways. Walking a mile is noticeably different from driving a mile. Today, we can physically circumnavigate the world in a little over forty-two hours. Yet in 1901, those three small dots signaled a distance and speed in communication technology that was unparalleled. Radio waves, a kind of electromagnetic radiation, travel at the speed of light, slightly under 300,000 kilometers per second. At that speed, Marconi's radio waves could go around the earth at the equator more than seven times per second.

So just a few seconds ago, the operator, with his imagined tea by his side, had pressed his keypad, and 2,200 miles away, Marconi had received the signals. It was a modern miracle, and Marconi took a moment to put his head down and send a brief prayer of thanks.

When Marconi released the information, the world reacted with a combination of awe, disbelief, congratulatory letters, splashed headlines, and gifts of lemon pound cake. He traveled to Ottawa and was treated like a king. He discovered tobogganing.

As he skimmed down the hill, the wind whipped his well-groomed hair so it stuck out on all sides. He had been in the company of three young debutantes, all of marriageable age, who had been thrust upon him by eager mothers. Thoughts of Josephine were left behind like ghosts falling away on the wind.

When Marconi arrived in New York, the newspapers were almost as interested in his love life as they were in the three dots sent across half the world. Everyone wanted to know, was the marriage off or on? He liked Josephine well enough. When they were together, he admired her intellectual abilities and the way the light gleamed off her auburn hair. But in his heart, he knew that something had changed. It had been a two-year courtship, and in those two years, they had been apart much more than together. Perhaps absence does not make the heart grow fonder. Maybe it just makes the heart forget.

He was let into Josephine's house by a servant whose cold indifference to him signaled much. Josephine made him wait for an hour and a half, and when she appeared in a peach taffeta dress at the top of the grand staircase, he knew it was completely over. He saw that she had been crying, for her face was patchy and her eyes red. He sat with her while she poured tea out of hand-painted tea cups. Violets, he thought. She was sipping tea demurely, calmly, but then she returned the cup so quickly to its saucer that both broke.

That sudden crash unleashed a torrent. She was beyond angry. Marconi gathered his hat and gloves and retreated past the eyes of her mother, who now stood in the foyer. The next day, front pages announced that the wedding was officially off.

Marconi plunged himself into managing his seventeen British outposts, his numerous New World stations, and his 130 patents. Deals were to be made with Lloyd's of London, the famous maritime insurance and information company, along with the Canadian government and the British. The Germans were to be watched carefully, as they were busy developing their own system that could be a threat to his own. His life became one of traveling, meetings, and interviewing. He never stopped.

Finally, he traveled to Glace Bay, a new station in Nova Scotia. The area was beautiful in a brutal way. The treeless cliffs were open to the rawness of the sweeping chill of the wind, perfect for hefting large kites into the sky. This was the site he had chosen to send a full sentence to the Old World. To Poldhu.

But what should he say? And to whom? This first communication would set the tone for the entire industry. He needed to be politically smart as well as socially astute. He decided to address the first missives to royalty. Recognizing the time zones, he timed the messages so they would all receive them at the same time. No one would be deemed better than the other for having received something earlier.

In preparation for the event, everyone put cotton wool in their ears, for the sounds of the sparks needed to send a message so far were deafening.

In the next few weeks, Marconi sent almost forty messages. Kings, queens, diplomats, presidents, premiers, and powerful businessmen all received wireless telegrams. This was not a seamless venture. Each message had to be sent over and over until it could finally be read at the receiving station.

The response was instantaneous. Everyone, whether vice presidents or viceroys, responded, extremely pleased to have made the short list on such a momentous occasion. Marconi had chosen well. Each telegram resonated throughout the press. It was as though the little bell he had rung so long ago at the Villa Griffone was now a giant gong, sending out waves of sound around the world.

Chapter Twenty-Three

INEZ: 1901

Marconi was not feeling well. He never had time to rest. Between running the business, managing the various stations, orchestrating government meetings, and keeping up with the press, there had been little time for sleep, much less any sustained breaks. The word "vacation" was one he didn't know.

The only time he could rest was on the steamships that took at least five days to cross the Atlantic. So he was relieved to be on one of his favorite ships, the RMS *Lucania*, among the fastest Cunard ships at the time. Irresistibly drawn to the engine room, he asked permission to tour it, and a sailor assigned the duty took him down to the bowels of the ship.

It was like taking a network of stairways to hell. The heat and noise were tremendous. The three engines were each 47 feet tall, about five decks, and reached almost from the bottom of the hull to the top deck. Each had five cylinders. When the ship was at full steam, it could go an average of 22 knots (about 25 miles) per hour. Marconi loved that raw feeling of mechanical power. It blew through his chest and somehow renewed him.

The engine room was in sharp contrast with the first-class dining saloon, Marconi's favorite place on the *Lucania*. After touring the engine room, he shaved and showered, put on his best evening clothes, and went in search of entertainment.

In the center of the 98-foot dining room was an area that reached up three decks. The soaring space ended in a white and gold ceiling supported by Ionic columns standing guard every 6 feet. The paneling was Spanish mahogany inlaid with ivory. Filigree rosettes, leaves, and an occasional cherub wound along the paneling.

A man in formal attire was playing a Steinway grand piano. When he took a break, Marconi sat down and played a piece from *Le disgrazie di un bel giovane, ossia il zio e il nipote*, an opera by Giuseppe Lillo, a little-known composer who wrote in the mid-1800s. He was swept back in time to rare occasions when his mother would take him to the Teatro Capranica, a small but elaborate opera house in Rome with exceptional acoustics. Annie would hum almost inaudibly to herself, and Marconi would wonder if she was regretting her chosen life.

Suddenly aware of a presence on his right, he looked over to see a dark-haired woman staring at him. Her face was lit from within with intensity, joy, and a life force that almost jarred him from the piano stool. She waited until the last notes had faded away before she grabbed his hand and kissed it. This was Inez Milholland, a seventeen-year-old, Brooklyn-born suffragist and social reformer.

Marconi was enraptured. Josephine had been a woman of the last century, someone who was proper and knew the social morals of the time. Inez pushed against them.

Their first meal together was a feast like none he had ever experienced. From the first sips of champagne to the last bites of chocolate mousse, it was an experience in perception. He parsed the food like a chemist would, each bite a complex series of salts and sugars. He felt the effects of everything he put in his mouth. It was all because of Inez. She existed in a field of observation. From that day on, he always maintained that she was the true scientist.

She savored everything, slowly bringing bites of roast duck to her mouth while never taking her eyes off him. She asked him how everything tasted and would not let him describe things simply. She demanded that he think deeply about what he was eating. She talked of flowers and the feel of satin, how a well-made dress felt on the skin. She talked of women's equality and made it sound like a recipe for men and women to work together on equal terms. Why not? They had the same sensory apparatus, the same tools. By the time they arrived at the mousse, Marconi had forgotten his tiredness. He was ready to talk until dawn.

The entire Atlantic crossing was a departure from his normal life. Languorous breakfasts of fluffy soufflés and small cups of buttered shrimp were followed by sun-drenched hours in the deck chairs as they held each other's hands and talked about what a simple cup of tea might be doing to the human brain.

By the time they docked in England, Marconi was in love. Inez's family were accepting and wealthy, and they began calling him "Billy." He was now managing to balance his work life with his romantic life, and he went often to the Milhollands' townhouse on the edge of Kensington Gardens.

The family was fascinated by Marconi and his invention. They spent hours over the dinner table expounding on civil rights, the responsibility of the media, prison reform, issues of race, and the suffragists. They sandwiched in conversations on technology, science, and the possibility of human flight.

For Marconi, it was a lesson in the new century. Here were people who saw the future and talked about it as though they would wake up tomorrow and find the world unalterably changed. They placed him squarely on the forefront of that change and welcomed him as a primary example. He was madly in love, and Inez was young, surprising, and had a bohemian family that appealed to him.

When he proposed to Inez, she accepted. He bathed in Inez's embrace and her family's praise for almost a year before waking up as though in a dream. Although he loved and respected Inez, he felt that she was not marriage material. He let her down with a last sumptuous meal at the Savoy. After the last licks of chocolate mousse were devoured, he told her. Two large tears fell down her cheeks. She blotted them with her linen napkin, took a sip of champagne, and asked him how long he thought it would take before women could vote.

Soon after, Marconi bought a Napier Roadster in coquelicot red with black trim. He learned to drive it from a man named Henry he met in Liverpool. Henry taught him not only how to drive, but everything about the mechanics of the car. Within a week, Marconi was taking the curves too fast.

Marconi was in London at Simpson's in the Strand. His roast beef had just arrived under its silver dome. The waiter was theatrically serving him his first slices, the juices dripping onto his plate, when the maître d' came to him, a telegram in hand. His father, Giuseppe Marconi, eighty years old, had died.

Marconi took a sip of wine. He ate a bit of bread. He stumbled out into the March air, found himself a carriage, and took to his bed in his Piccadilly suite.

He arrived at his mother's apartments the next morning to find her already dressed in black, her face a stiff oval in white. They collapsed into each other's arms while the rest of the family gathered at Palazzo Albergati in Bologna, where Giuseppe had been wintering.

Everyone, including Marconi, was amazed to learn that, going against all Italian traditions, Giuseppe had bequeathed Villa Griffone not to his eldest son but his youngest. Guglielmo, the child who had gone head-to-head with him most often, had received the place of his father's heart.

Chapter Twenty-Four

It was a year of traipsing around the world. Now Marconi was truly a magician and juggler, for he could keep a host of spinning plates in the air. One of his many stations was at Haven in Poole Harbour, a 6-mile train ride from London. Haven was one of his favorites. The weather was on the calm side, and the North Haven Inn, run by a couple by the name of Poulain, set a fine French table.

At Haven, Marconi had made friends with the van Raaltes, a wealthy Dutch family who had taken over nearby Brownsea Island, where they were renovating an old castle. Marconi loved all things that spoke of royalty, and all brushes with royal families. When they invited him to visit, he accepted. A castle seemed like the perfect place to rest, and besides, the van Raaltes were said to be witty hosts who knew their wines.

When the ferry ended its 5-mile journey from the coast at Poole Harbour to the cove on Brownsea Island, he was pleased to see a crenellated castle fit for any Anglican king. Henry VIII had built it around 1546 to protect the coast from invasion. Now the van Raaltes were transforming it, creating thirty-eight bedrooms for their guests and an elaborate music room to house their collection of 250 musical instruments.

As soon as the hawsers were tied, Marconi leaped from the ferry like any seasoned sailor. He was making his way up the gravel path toward the castle when he saw her. Beatrice O'Brien, with her long hair curling down along her left shoulder, was coming down the stone path to the boat ramp as though she was walking down the red carpet at Buckingham Palace. Framed by the wisteria, which twined up and along the pergola, and with the castle in the background, she looked like a princess from one of Marconi's childhood picture books.

Indeed, she was close, for Beatrice was the daughter of Lord and Lady Inchiquin of Dromoland Castle in County Clare, Ireland. Marconi, a foreigner and inventor, was smitten with someone from the peerage. This was a new problem he needed to solve, and he went about it in the same way he approached all problems. He strategized, thinking about it from every angle. He decided he would actively woo her.

Bea, as she was known, was a consummate whist player. Marconi soon became one, too. She could often be found in the music room. So could he. He was witty, urbane, and, fortunately, he had been raised by his mother as a Protestant, not a Catholic. He found a co-conspirator in his hostess, Florence van Raalte. She was a tall, good-looking woman with a nose that spoke of kings. She took great interest in Marconi and Beatrice and became a critical player in his campaign to win her.

Bea was a late sleeper and usually had breakfast in the main room at eleven. By then, Marconi had walked the grounds, had a breakfast of hot chocolate and croissants, and sent his daily telegrams. He would bump into Bea as though by accident, feigning looking for a friend or a book. Bea would smirk and they both would laugh. They became friends. Marconi wanted more.

Bea was the opposite of Inez. She was regal, well bred, and knew how women of the times, especially women of importance, were supposed to behave. (When Inez heard of the flirtation, she commented that Beatrice looked to her like "some kind of dinky-doo.") Once, when Marconi offered to drive Bea to town, she refused, based on the impropriety of riding alone with him while unmarried.

Marconi was intrigued by something he could not have. He had always responded to impediments with strength, and here was an impediment in human form. He made sure he knew where she was at most times, and contrived to be at a charity ball at Albert Hall on the same night she was.

When she came down the ballroom staircase, he intercepted her, knelt, and proposed. Bea was clearly taken aback. She raised her oriental fan and covered her mouth. He stood and said she could think about it, and he would call on her in a few days.

When he called on her at her London apartments, she was distraught. She sat him down on a striped divan and fed him tea and crumpets without saying a word. He, on the other hand, couldn't seem to stop talking and blathered away about boats, swans, and the benefits of hunting.

Finally, after it was clear that neither of them could tolerate drinking even one more sip of tea, she began talking. Her speech would be recognizable to many modern men. She told him that although she liked him, she didn't love him. That she did not feel that way about him but that she only considered him a good friend. The answer was a kind but emphatic no.

~

Marconi threw himself into his work. As usual, he traveled. While in New York, he took to driving his roadster through the streets of Lower Manhattan and once was pulled over for speeding. The *Halifax Herald* reported seeing him with a lovely woman in a red dress. He visited each of his stations, had meetings with the American branch of his company, and dined with many women.

Although the press enjoyed making much of it, Marconi made little of his friendship with Alice Roosevelt, the eldest child of President Theodore Roosevelt. He claimed that he visited her for business and political reasons. In private, he found her an interesting friend, a social rebel, and a bit of a snob. Whenever he went to see her, he prepared for an unusual encounter.

Alice was smoking a cigarette. Marconi did not think he had even seen anyone enjoy one more. They were in her apartments on the Upper West Side of Manhattan. She was wearing one of her "Alice blue" dresses, a bright blue that for a time was a national trend. Leo, her Chihuahua, was asleep in her lap. Coiled around her left arm was her pet garter snake, Emily Spinach, and she held a French Lillet aperitif in her right hand. Marconi wondered how she balanced everything all at once.

Alice was pontificating about America's first bodybuilding competition, where she had seen strongman Al Treloar. She took a long drag on her cigarette and commented that he was, as billed, "The Most Perfectly Developed Man in the World." Marconi was in no mood to talk about other men. He left before she could insist that he hold Emily.

~

Christmas was coming. Although Marconi was not entirely a religious man, he enjoyed the holiday, and there was no better place to be for Christmas than Brownsea Island. The van Raaltes took out all the stops, and the castle hummed like an organ. Among the garlands and pine trees, lights, and plum puddings, the van Raaltes presented music. On each night of December, a different band, quartet, consort, choral group, ensemble, octet, chamber orchestra, quintet, or septet played or sang, and it all culminated on Christmas Eve with a full-sized orchestra.

Marconi wrote to Florence to see if she could lure Bea to Brownsea. Florence replied that she would do what she could. When Bea expressly asked if Marconi would be there, Florence lied and said no. So Bea came.

Marconi had a plan. He asked Florence if he could play a small interlude on the piano on Christmas Eve. If the orchestra was willing to accompany him, so much the better. He passed out their parts a month in advance and rehearsed in secret in London.

On December 24, 1904, the great hall had never looked better. The soaring two-story ceiling twinkled with candlelight, and fresh garlands of fir perfumed the air. Marconi peeked out at the fifty or so people and immediately spied Bea, her back straight, her gaze steady and thoughtful. She had never looked more beautiful.

When the orchestra finished the first selection of the night, Marconi took the stage and sat down at the Bösendorfer grand piano. Voices murmured. Before starting to play, he simply announced, "'Divertimento for Piano, Violins and Cello in C Major' by Haydn. For Beatrice." When he finished, the waves of clapping seemed to go on for several minutes. He looked over at Bea and saw that her eyes were locked on his.

This time, when he proposed, she gave him a qualified yes. If her sister Lilah agreed, then she would, too. Both women agreed.

The next rampart to overcome was his mother. When Marconi and Bea entered Annie's house, they found her ensconced in her sitting room, holding court like a queen. She had already been through this once with Josephine. She knew she could make it difficult for her son, if not impossible. If she wanted to stand in the way of this marriage, she certainly could.

But the minute the rumors had reached her ears, she had started her own investigations. Did Guglielmo look happy when he and Beatrice were together? Was she from a good family? Was she raised as a good Protestant? Did she believe in children? Were there any scandals attached to her name or to her family? Who were her parents? Were they drunks? How many sisters did she have? Brothers?

Annie's thoroughness would have put any academic researcher to shame. She used every connection she knew to get a full portrait of Beatrice in advance. By the time they met, she felt she knew her. When Bea walked into the room, Annie offered her a cup of hot tea, a warm scone, and a glowing smile. She had already passed the test.

Guglielmo Marconi and Beatrice O'Brien were married on March 16, 1905, at St. George's Church in Hanover Square in central London. Both families had wanted a quiet wedding, but it was not to be. The morning of the sixteenth, Marconi woke early and finished up some correspondence, reread a contract, and sent twenty-two telegrams. He then donned a Lombard silk vest, a silk puff tie, black Henderson trousers, a cutaway coat, and a John Bull top hat. When he arrived at the church, more than a thousand people were milling around outside. Even more surprising was the group of English bobbies who were plunging through the door. Word had gotten around that someone's life was being threatened. The police scoured the church and concluded the threat was a hoax.

Marconi's nerves were on edge, and he knew he had a slight fever. He sent a message to Bea that he hoped would calm her down. In fact, she was quite calm. Her maid was helping to seal her up in her wedding dress by completing the fifty-first button loop in the back. Bea stood before the full-length mirror and cocked her head. She could hear the rumblings of the crowd outside the church. She could smell honeycomb wax candles and cold earthiness from the old stone walls. Her heart was clear. She would marry Marconi and care for him.

The marriage ceremony went without any problems from either crowds or killers. The newlyweds fled the church in an open Victoria French carriage and began their honeymoon at her family's estate in Ireland, Dromoland. They found the castle drafty, nearly deserted, dark, and depressing. Marconi took long walks alone, his chest leaden with the mist and damp. Bea sat in the massive library, her face bowed over a book she was not reading.

It was a relief to be on the RMS *Campania* on the way to New York. The day they left, it was bright and calm. The porters brought everything up to their airy stateroom, and it wasn't until Marconi started unpacking clocks that Bea became a little worried. As he placed them around the room, he explained that his business had become so complex he needed to know what time it was in twenty different time zones. Bea thought the ticking would drive her mad. The only cure was to stuff her ears with cotton.

Another quirk became apparent the second day at sea. She walked in to find Marconi throwing clothes out of the port window. He must be wealthy, she thought, as he explained that throwing clothes away was easier than laundering them.

But Bea knew that part of marriage was getting to know the eccentricities of one's partner, becoming used to them, and forgiving them. She could do these things before the cruise was over.

New York was a series of parties. They dined with Grace Vanderbilt, whose elopement with her new husband, Cornelius, had almost cost her every family dime. President Roosevelt and Alice, who for once kept her cigarettes and her bon mots well hidden away from her father, invited them up to their summer estate in Oyster Bay, where they had a lunch of oysters Rockefeller. ("Oysters at Oyster Bay," Alice remarked before sucking one down). They enjoyed being feted by numerous overstuffed bankers, bejeweled socialites, and one scrawny, dyspeptic prince.

In among these social events, Marconi received the welcome news that after three years of legal process, he had won his patent case. He now ruled the seas and the land, for the Marconi system had beaten out all other contenders and was ruled the original wireless system.

The parties proved eye-opening for Bea. There was not a breakfast, lunch, dinner, soiree, or tea without a mixed reason for their presence, for Marconi was a master at combining business with pleasure. After the chatter about art, music, and society had faded away, the talk always turned to business.

They traveled to Glace Bay, where Marconi disappeared into the gaping maw of his outpost. Bea, installed in the hotel, whiled away the hours with books, knitting, and eating chocolates. She gained three pounds. A honeymoon of loneliness is a bitter thing.

Although it was April, she bundled up to take even a short stroll along the craggy coastline. The wind was an icy blade that cut through her when the flap of her coat opened. She rarely saw Marconi, and when she did, his head was usually buried in charts, maps, and legal documents.

She witnessed how, when he ran a fever, he left the window open at night so ice formed on the pitcher. She saw how he combed his hair with pomade and left his toenails on the bathroom floor. In short, the honeymoon was over, and married life, with its bodily functions and the demands of the world, became the norm.

They returned to England and she found herself in Poldhu, another outpost far from the comforts of London society. Marconi installed her in the hotel, and once again, time weighed her down like a chunk of granite.

One day in June, Bea was in the hotel's limited library, tracing her finger along the well-worn copies of Dickens's *Oliver Twist*, Stendhal's *Le Rouge et le Noir* (The Red and the Black), and *A Polite Mother's Dictionary of Words Suitable for Children* when she was suddenly overcome with nausea. She took to her bed, thinking the hotel's tasteless food had finally gotten to her. Instead, she was pregnant.

Chapter Twenty-Five

For Bea, the world now became a series of bad smells. Kippers, bangers, and fried eggs made her turn a delicate shade of green. Although Marconi was ecstatic about being a prospective father, his time was spent out in the field or in the company office. Bea could keep nothing down. At times like these, there is nothing like one's mother, so they agreed that Bea should travel to London and spend the rest of her pregnancy with her family.

The day of her journey dawned softly, and for once, Bea kept toast down. As Marconi helped her into the closed carriage, she felt a wave of love waft over her. He had been mostly absent for the past month, but moments of intimacy had bound them together. When he was in the right mood, he would play Chopin for her, and the small music room in the hotel became a place of familiarity and warmth. He easily made his way through intricate arpeggios, his hands nimbly ebbing and flowing up and down the keyboard. He would look at her with his bright, intelligent eyes, and she would melt a bit inside, so when he led her up to their small room, there was no need for any more mood setting.

As he closed the carriage door, he gave her a small military salute, a gesture that had become an endearing joke between them. Then he told the driver to drive on.

Bea took up residence at 34 Charles Street in London— close to her mother, yet far enough away to feel as though she was a woman on her own. She furnished the house in the style of the day, with a Thomas Sheraton living room set, René Lalique glassware, and Tiffany lighting. The house felt light and full of air.

On February 4, Bea felt a roaring surge and knew that she was going into labor. Marconi was at Poldhu and a telegram was quickly dispatched. Her mother was sent for, water was boiled, and the doctor stood by as Bea delivered a beautiful baby girl with Marconi's dark hair and blue eyes.

As Bea stared at this new being, she knew that marriage to Marconi had been the right thing to do. She was destined to be a mother all along. The baby wrapped her index finger with her small hand, and Bea was at peace in a way she had never been before.

Bea had done the baby's room in yellow. Baby elephants, kangaroos, and donkeys in pastel colors pranced across the walls. Weeks after the birth, Bea and Marconi stood together, looking at Lucia, asleep in her lacy and beribboned cradle. The sun was warm through the window, and a wren sang in the tree outside. Marconi took Bea's hand and held it.

Suddenly, Lucia began to shudder. She arched her back. Her small face, ringed with curls of black hair, grimaced with pain, then stilled. Marconi and Bea had not moved. The room was just as it had been minutes before. The sun shone and the bird sang. But Lucia no longer breathed.

Marconi, stricken in a way he had never believed possible, took to his bed with a high fever. He dreamed of home. Villa Griffone was a dark, unwelcoming castle, and the fields were filled with ogres and witches from his childhood storybooks. His breath wheezed in and out of him, as if his lungs were faulty bagpipes.

Bea, also overcome with grief, took comfort in nursing Marconi. She applied cold compresses to his brow and rubbed his ice-cold feet.

Marconi wrote to his mother with the awful news that she would never see her first grandchild. "I am sure she is singing with the angels," he wrote, "in a voice like yours." When Annie received the letter, she was at Villa Griffone. She stared out at the gray fields. Far away on the horizon, a flock of crows flew by like stippled pencil points. She dropped the letter in her lap and cried.

Several years earlier, Marconi had contracted malaria somewhere in Montenegro. It came roaring back, complete with splitting headaches, chills, sweats, and vomiting. Marconi couldn't raise his head without it spinning. Though the workload continued to pile up, he was incapable of answering a single letter. His staffs around the world were forced to step up, put off what they could, and deal with anything that would stop their work.

To amuse himself, Marconi started collecting medical ads and railing against the inefficiencies that had allowed his daughter to die and himself to remain bedridden. He once threw an empty chamber pot at the attending physician and was known to throw anything within reach in a pique of frustration. Every evening, after Marconi finally succumbed to sleep, Bea quietly removed all objects, including books, pens, and teacups, from his bedside table.

Finally, three months later, Marconi's malaria was under control, his grief had subsided, and his general health was at a level where he could ease back into his former nonstop schedule of meetings, travel, and clambering around various antennas trying to understand why they weren't working. Bea stayed in London and tried to recover from the death of her daughter and the sleep she had lost while attending to her demanding patient.

Marconi was relieved when an ongoing dispute with his manager, H. Cuthbert Hall, was finally resolved and Hall lost out in a classic boardroom scuffle. This allowed Marconi to hire someone new. Godfrey Charles Isaac was a man who knew business. He would take the Marconi company, shake it by the tail, and force it to at last become an entity that made money. Marconi would finally be able to focus on research, the thing he liked best.

Glace Bay proved to be the best medicine for Marconi. The bracing weather and the constant problem-solving meant that he could put the months of sadness and sickness behind him. Dressed in tennis flannels, lumberjack boots, and a cabled sweater, he tried to work on a new problem: how to send and receive at the same time. This was the kind of problem he loved. He just had to tinker and think, think and tinker, until the two activity modes came together in a solution.

Bea and her sister Eileen came to visit him in Glace Bay. These stations were remote by necessity. They needed space and quiet, and they needed to be within a stone's throw of the coast. The O'Brien sisters took the RMS *Empress of Ireland*, a beautiful steamer with double smokestacks, shiny black sides, and a red hull, to Rimouski, Quebec. After a twelve-hour train ride that included two drunks being booted off the train and one flock of stubborn sheep on the tracks, they disembarked at the small depot in Glace Bay.

As Bea and Eileen left the train, they noticed that their hair was standing on end. A storm was brewing, coming in from the north. It hit just after they made it to the carriage that was waiting for them. Bea peered out at the darkening landscape and saw a deep green forest on both sides of the road. The flashes of lightning made the forest appear white, and she gripped her sister's arms. When they arrived at the station, men were standing at the windows looking up at the antenna towers worried that they would attract a strike.

Marconi, a fearful expression on his face, gave Bea a peck on the cheek and turned back to the window. All eyes were on the antenna. It wasn't until the storm passed that he turned to the two women, brought them tea, and welcomed them.

Bea found that she liked Nova Scotia. Although at times the mosquitoes seemed big enough to carry her away, being outdoors was a tonic. She especially enjoyed fishing for salmon. Her brother Barney was working for Marconi by now, and he showed her how to bait her hook and wait for the silvery fish to swim upstream. The Norwegian pines framed the stream, and she sometimes took off her stockings and waded into water that was so cold her feet ached.

It was easy to put the death of her first child into a small pocket of her mind. Especially when she learned that she was pregnant again.

Chapter Twenty-Six

DEGNA: 1908

On the way back to London, Bea and Marconi enjoyed being a couple. Bea's sister Eileen, two years younger than Bea, flirted with the officers. When she dropped her handkerchief on the ground for a young unsuspecting ensign, Marconi's eyes met Bea's, and they shared a private moment. Marconi saluted her, and she saluted back.

This pregnancy was unlike the first. Bea felt as though eating a horse would not be enough. For breakfast, she dined on quail eggs, English Breakfast tea, and crumpets. Lunch was tea sandwiches, watercress soup, and Westminster salad. During dinner, she was so ravenous she would finish Marconi's and Eileen's plates as well as her own. She felt robust and rosy.

Marconi, wanting his wife to retain those good feelings, rented a beautiful country house in southern England called Somborne Park. Bea settled in like a hen on her nest. She summered the months away taking long walks through open fields and listening to meadowlarks.

Meanwhile, Marconi was busy connecting Glace Bay with a new station at Clifden in Ireland. The plan was to start a commercial wireless telegraph service between the two stations.

Godfrey Isaac had put the plan together, and Marconi was relieved to finally have a person in place who could figure out a way to make the business profitable.

After the blossoming summer months, Marconi and Bea agreed that she needed to be in town for the birth, so they rented a comfortable house on George Street in London. Bea was sorry to say goodbye to her pastoral existence, but she recognized from experience that birth, like any other natural process, was open to chance, miracles, and disasters.

Marconi was needed at Glace Bay, so he made the trip across the ocean yet again.

On September 11, 1908, Bea gave birth to a daughter. Two days earlier, Orville Wright flew for an hour in Virginia, and Marconi sent Bea a telegram with the headline "Orville Wright Breaks World Flying Records." Now Bea was flying high as well. Tempered by the knowledge that anything could go wrong, she soaked up the smell of her new daughter like it was liquid roses. When Marconi finally came back to join her, they christened her Degna, an old Italian name meaning "worthy."

Marconi could scarcely afford paternity time off, and once they named the child and he had spent a few days in London, he left for Ireland to see how things were at Clifden.

Bea and little Degna went back to Somborne Park. Fall was as beautiful there as the summer had been, but this time Bea had Degna to share it with. She kept the heavy black pram just inside the kitchen door so they could easily escape to the freshened fall air, and they went on walks that lasted almost the entire day.

Bea understood that in many ways, Marconi needed her. Although they saw each other rarely, she was important to him in terms of stability and family, and how he viewed himself. He was a complicated man at a complicated juncture in history. On the one hand, he was a product of old-time Italy, a world made up of grains and grapes, olive trees and figs. On the other, his life was filled with travel, technology, and smart, sophisticated, modern people.

He wrote to her often, calling her a pet name, "Buzzel." He told her he was well and thriving; that his lungs were a little raspy; that the Clifden aerials were giving them trouble. He apologized for not being there and hoped to see her and their little daughter soon. He sent his love.

Over the next few years, Marconi crisscrossed the Atlantic so many times that he sometimes felt like the messages he was sending. On January 23, 1909, he was on board the RMS *Republic*, nicknamed "the Millionaires' Ship" because it carried the wealthiest clientele. Run by the White Star line, the ship was outfitted with luxury suites, multiple ballrooms, and wide promontory decks.

She was headed toward the warming seas of the Mediterranean. Most of the 1,200 passengers were still inside, avoiding the early morning fog that blanketed the decks and the watery expanse beyond. The foghorns blared every five minutes, reminding people as they began to wake up or lay in bed that they were indeed at sea. Breakfasts were being made, people were yawning, and children were beginning to stir when they felt a staggering jolt and heard the sickening screech of metal on metal.

Soon the *Republic* listed to one side. It had been rammed by the SS *Florida*, an Italian liner en route to Nantucket. Shrill whistles split the air as people hastily grabbed their children and their jewels and hurried out on deck.

One man did not run out onto the deck. He was the wireless operator, recently installed by the Marconi company, and his name was John R. Binns. People called him Jack. He was twenty-four and full of punch. A Protestant with dark, serious eyes, Jack took responsibility like he owned it, like it was his only child. He didn't drink or smoke, and he attended services on Sundays in the ship's oak-walled chapel.

The second the collision occurred, Jack started sending out CQDs, the Marconi Morse code distress signals. He had immediately recognized what had happened, and he knew that every second counted. As passengers began flooding the decks, he stayed in the radio room. At first, it seemed that no one could hear him. He leaned into the desk and tapped out the code again and again. Wasn't anyone awake? Wasn't anyone listening?

It felt like hours, but within minutes, the US Coast Guard Cutter *Gresham* was on its way to the rescue. The cutter was a small ship, designed to intercept smugglers, and could not take even half of the 1,200 people who needed to be rescued. Fortunately, the SS *Florida* was unharmed and could back away from the *Republic* and come alongside to make the transference of the passengers easier.

Surprisingly, no one panicked. Perhaps it was the fact that it was early morning and they were still not fully awake, or perhaps it was the reassuring presence of the other ships, but passengers filed onto the *Florida* and the *Gresham* like they were walking down a path in Central Park. Panic is a social contagion, and it wasn't until a third ship arrived that a riot broke out.

The ship was the *Baltic*, another White Star luxury liner, and the riot was the result of the class system. People from steerage were forced to wait until all the remaining first-class passengers had been transported to the *Baltic* before they were allowed to board. When children from the lower decks were forced to wait for the transfer of wealthy bankers and their wives, their fathers and mothers began shouting, pushing, and shoving. Money and prestige now became a hardened reality: your life and the lives of your children were not deemed as valuable as those wrapped in fur coats against the chill.

It took a major effort by the officers and sailors to calm everyone down, and it wasn't until the upper classes had been removed that the lower classes were allowed onto the *Baltic*. The sympathetic staff settled them in brocaded Windsor chairs in front of the fireplaces or bedded them down in the watered silk walled suites and fed them whiskey and cocoa.

Only six people lost their lives, and their deaths were due to the collision itself. This miracle of 1,194 saved lives was claimed by the new Marconi wireless system. Stock soared.

Chapter Twenty-Seven

AWARDED: 1909

The world recognized Marconi for what he was: a man who had changed the scope and scale of the planet, who could be counted among the movers and shakers of the time. In 1909, he finally got the formal recognition he craved. He won the Nobel Prize in Physics, sharing it with German inventor Karl Ferdinand Braun "in recognition of their contributions to the development of wireless telegraphy."

Marconi and Bea traveled to Stockholm, stepping from a closed carriage onto Södra Blasieholmshamnen, the snowy street in front of the palatial Grand Hôtel Royal. It was December, and the wind sweeping off Lake Malaren carried the lake's icy depths. They hurried into one of the most opulent hotels they had ever seen.

Throughout the week of festivities, Bea gravitated toward the hotel's new Winter Garden. This immense atrium, filled with green palms, wicker tables, and glass animal sculptures, was an antidote to the freezing weather outside and a brainchild of the hotel's director, Wilhelmina Skogh. Wilhelmina was a stout, loud Norwegian whose claim to fame was the ability to make people laugh within two minutes of meeting her. Every morning, Bea sought her out during the relative quiet of midday near one of the saw-toothed palms planted in the central gallery.

Wilhelmina poured strong tea and told stories about the smartest people in the world, who gathered each year in Stockholm to receive their prestigious awards. The literary, scientific, and medical geniuses of the world were also people who had splendid accidents. She told wonderful stories of the doctor who broke a precious vase with his sword, the economist who broke his ankle when demonstrating a pirouette, and the chemist who fell asleep under the piano. Bea laughed more during that week than she had for the past year.

The week culminated with the awards ceremony. Marconi and Bea sat in the grand ballroom among people the world regarded as the best and the brightest. The twenty-one chandeliers illuminated the men in their black suits and the women in their peacock-colored dresses of blues, greens, and golds.

Years after, Bea remembered only one speech: that of Selma Lagerlöf, the first woman to win the Nobel Prize in Literature. It was memorable because it was so unusual. Lagerlöf, unlike most wives in the room, wore black. She was heavy and squat, yet her personality was so gentle, so filled with a quiet, almost unheard joke, that she charmed the entire room.

Her speech was a story. She told of knocking on the gates of heaven and finding her father in a cozy cottage, his feet up on a red ottoman, smoking a pipe. He offered her peppermint candies in a dish made of gold, and as she warmed her hands on the fire, he told her that she had incurred a debt. She was a bit shocked, and he helped her sit down in a chair in front of the fireplace. He explained quietly and lovingly that the debt was due to the people who had helped her. Her mother, her family, even the village butcher all played some role in helping her to this spot, this moment in time, in front of everyone in this beautiful hotel.

Bea dabbed at her eyes. Lagerlöf's speech was a poetic counterpoint to the men who stood and spoke. Marconi joined the ranks and spent fifteen minutes droning on about his invention, his world of wires and wireless.

It wasn't until the last minute that she started truly listening. It was then that Marconi painted a picture of the future. He envisioned a time when electrical impulses would span the globe—when people could talk to their Italian grandmothers halfway around the world, when American doctors could talk to their patients in Ireland, when ships at sea were always connected to the land. And all of it would cost next to nothing.

As Marconi returned to his seat, Bea squeezed his hand. Sometimes she forgot about this side of her husband, this visionary side. Marconi squeezed her hand in return, and for a moment their eyes met. It was a rare moment when they both let the world fade away. Beatrice would remember it for years.

By the time Marconi returned to Glace Bay, the weather was raw and the men cranky from their weather-enforced captivity. Marconi sipped his customary mug of cocoa and contemplated a problem. So far, messages could only be sent one at a time, one way—a simplex system. In his mind, he was working out a way that messages could be sent and received at the same time—a duplex system. This could be done with a smaller apparatus and perhaps require different stations. As Marconi stared out the window at the complex and expensive system that reached up into the gray skies, he envisioned finding yet another site for this new idea that would allow him to compete even more effectively with the wire companies.

Within two years, he had two more stations: Louisbourg, about 20 miles from Glace Bay, and Letterfrack near Clifden in Ireland. The building of these stations had taken up much of his time.

In Ireland, the issue was tenants. There were families who had worked the land in that area for hundreds of years. Each tenant had to be individually wooed, and Marconi, with his respect for the working man, painstakingly met with each until they were all behind the idea of living with a field of antennas next to their fields of wheat.

In Canada, the issue was weather. Old-timers had spoken of hundred-year winters when the land hadn't thawed until July and the crops season was so short that people starved.

When Marconi arrived at Glace Bay, there had been so much sleet and ice that the station was in a state of alert. Men with ankle-length coats, binoculars, and wool caps pulled over their ears were positioned so they could watch the antennas from all sides. Everyone knew that "silver thaws," as they were called, could pull down trees, so they watched with fear as the storm weighed the antenna down until it was close to the breaking point.

The antennas at Glace Bay survived, but the land lines connecting Glace Bay to the new station at Louisbourg did not. Marconi was in the field with his men in the early gray morning when the wires silently fell. It was as though all sound had stopped, for the snow had covered the land with a mound of cotton batting.

As Marconi gazed at the wires, now lying on the ground, the sun came out, transforming the landscape into a fairytale. The bright red flit of a cardinal was like a splash of blood, for everything else was white and silver. The skeletal oak trees were sculptures made of molten metal. Warmed by the sun, the ice dripped into icicles as tall as a ten-year-old.

For Marconi, this was just another impediment made for him to climb over. His pragmatism and optimism fed the men like hot soup. Within three months, the wires had been restrung, and Marconi had successfully sent and received messages simultaneously from across the ocean.

Winter in New York means that your overcoat is never warm enough, because the wind cuts through the streets like a knife. Marconi was happy when he finally arrived at Delmonico's. The doorman, dressed in red, greeted Marconi as usual, with a salute. Marconi, brushing snow off the shoulders of his coat, did not notice the woman behind him until she suddenly put her hands over his eyes.

He turned to see Inez Milholland, looking chic in a diaphanous plum-colored gown. Laughing at his expression of mild shock, she linked her arm in his and led him to her table, which was filled with the bohemian set from Greenwich Village.

Inez had not been idle since they had called off their engagement. She was now in her twenties and a fixture in the American feminist movement. Her trademark political action was to take her white mare, Gray Dawn, and lead the suffragist parades down Pennsylvania Avenue. Wearing a crown topped by a star, she did not ride sidesaddle, like most women of her time, but instead rode astride her horse, like a man. She approached life in the same way—head on.

Marconi plunged into this set of characters like a drowning man finding land. George Melies, a French filmmaker, sat on his right and performed card tricks. A woman named François kept setting up her spoons so that when she pounded on them, they would fly through the air and strike the man sitting opposite. Inez had brought books she was cutting into strips, and the man beside her was burning holes in the tablecloth with his cigarette. Marconi ordered an aperitif and settled down to reacquaint himself with the artists and writers of the day.

At the end of the evening, Inez shed her companions, and she and Marconi settled into comfortable leather chairs to catch up. Inez was studying law and had managed to get herself arrested multiple times while supporting the Triangle Shirtwaist Factory workers. She was a passionate advocate of good education, and she described the new ideas put forth by Maria Montessori, an Italian doctor who had opened a school called the Casa dei Bambini (Children's House) in a low-income district of Rome.

Marconi, for once not the most vocal person at the table, wondered how different his life would be if he had married Inez rather than Bea. He decided that Inez was like a fire that burned brightly—nice to be near on a cold night, but not necessarily in all seasons. When they parted, she gave him a peck on the cheek and pinched it for good measure.

Chapter Twenty-Eight

Bea had a wonderful idea that, in retrospect, turned out to be a terrible idea. She would take a skiff out to meet the transatlantic ship that she knew carried Marconi. She would leave from Cork Harbor and surprise him with the news that she was pregnant for the third time.

As her little boat came along the tall outer hull of the RMS *Olympic*, she had a moment of doubt, but she shrugged off the feeling that had landed briefly between her shoulder blades.

When she entered the music room, a party was in full swing. The great tenor Enrico Caruso was singing *Porquoi me réveiller?* (Why wake me?), and Marconi was playing the grand piano. The room was a riot of silk, taffeta, lace, and tulle. Creamy ecrus, glistening golds, and vibrant reds swished and swayed. The room was full of women.

As Bea came in, it was as though a stone had been thrown into a pond. She walked to the center of the room where the piano was, and the colorful dresses withdrew to the outer walls. Only Caruso and Marconi remained. Caruso faded out in mid-note, and Marconi turned to see why.

When he saw Bea, his face darkened with anger. He rose slowly, pushing the piano bench back with his knee. Holding her firmly by the elbow, he hurried her out of the room.

The second the door closed behind them, Marconi started hissing at her, asking her why she had come. When she told him she was pregnant, he began yelling. People in the hallway glanced back after passing by. He began pacing, telling her it could not possibly be his.

Bea was shocked and sickened. For a moment, she stood there, letting his voice wash over her. Then she abruptly turned and walked down the hall, not looking back. It wasn't until she had located Marconi's stateroom that she completely crumpled.

After the steward let her in, she collapsed on the bed and cried until she was empty of tears. She splashed water on her face, straightened her skirt, and put a book in her lap. How often had she stared at books without reading them? She realized that a good part of her married life had been spent with an unread book open in her lap. The thought warmed her, and a straight shot of unadulterated rage coursed through her.

When Marconi finally came into the room to apologize, she did not throw anything. She did not hit him, slap him, or kick him in the shins, although she wanted to do all those things. Instead, she sat there while he made excuses for his behavior: not enough sleep, too much rich food, too busy, too distracted, too too. She had heard it all before. When he invited her back to the party, she simply stared at him.

When the ship docked, she was one of the first people to disembark. She swept down the gangplank without looking back. She took a carriage back to her London apartments and played with one-year-old Degna. She, for one, could count. She was pregnant with Marconi's child. She alone knew that to be true.

Chapter Twenty-Nine

THE UNSINKABLE SHIP: 1912

Marconi was swamped. Paperwork, his nemesis, surrounded him like a flat white army. He felt as though he was drowning in it. He yearned to chuck it all in the wastebin. It would feel as though a weight had been taken off. For a moment, he took the time to fully imagine what that would be like. The bin would overflow with receipts, contracts, weather reports, telegrams, maps, reports, letters of appreciation, letters of complaint, and a wrapper from the fish and chips shop around the corner.

He crumpled the wrapper, pitched it in, and sighed. It would be alone for a while until he could plow through the stacks. He had so wanted to participate in the maiden voyage of the great ship. So many people of importance were going: bankers, doctors, lawyers, financiers. It would have been good for business.

But the White Star's new star in the constellation of beautiful luxury liners would have to sail without him. The RMS *Titanic* would not have Guglielmo Marconi. But perhaps Bea and the children could go anyway. He would take an earlier ship and meet them in London.

～

Beatrice sat in the rocking chair next to Giulio's bed. Her two-year-old was sleeping restlessly. His face was flushed and his breathing raspy. Beatrice knew from first experience that children could die in the blink of an eye, and she would do everything she possibly could to make sure she never lost another child. She put the back of her hand against Giulio's forehead. He was too hot.

She did two things. First, she called her maid and asked her to locate a doctor. Second, she asked the butler to send a telegram: "The Marconi family sends its regrets, but it cannot participate in the maiden voyage of the *Titanic*."

They could, however, watch it leave Southampton.

Bea often felt that Eaglehurst, the country estate they rented, was her husband's consolation prize for not being around. She and the children roamed the grounds like waifs lost in a storm. Bea loved the wrens and robins, but the peacocks installed by prior occupants had to go. They were loud, arrogant, and bad luck, due to their "evil eye" feathers.

The estate included a three-story tower built by Temple Luttrell, a member of Parliament. Its official name was Luttrell's Tower, but the locals called it the Folly. It was rumored that Luttrell had used it as a smuggling center.

On April 10, 1912, Bea and Degna climbed the tower to the widow's walk. The climb was up a spiral staircase, and Bea felt old following the scampering Degna. When they went through the small white door and reached the circular balcony, she was glad they had come. The 360-degree panorama included the mansard rooftops, the towering elm trees, and the entire harbor, which lay before them like a crystal blue glove.

The *Titanic* was departing with horns, whistles, and bells. A tender April wind brought the scent of lilacs and roses. The town had come out to see the ship off, and she could faintly hear people yelling, perhaps saying "Bon voyage!"

As she and her mother mounted the stairs, four-year-old Degna was both excited and sad, for she knew they had been planning to ride the big boat across the ocean. But when they emerged on the balcony, she, too, was happy to be on such a high place with such a view, watching the ship down the harbor.

Bea sighed. Oh, to be a child again, when the happiness of now always took over the unhappiness of yesterday! She knew that no one on board the *Titanic* could see her, but she took the handkerchief from the neck of her dress and waved it in the air. Degna added her own celebratory hoots.

It would have been so wonderful to be on board, Bea thought. To share the experience with so many good friends. She could have shown off her new Parisian dress and her new baby. She could have dressed Degna in her silk dress with the bows. She could have shown Guglielmo just how smart, witty, and urbane she could be.

She would have sipped champagne, but not too much. She would have eaten foie gras and mussels, although both were foreign to her. She would have danced the new dances—the Cakewalk, the Mazurka, and the Hesitation Waltz. Marconi would have looked at her with love in his eyes.

She turned away from the sight of the steaming *Titanic*. What she had in front of her was much more important than the frivolity of dancing. She had a sick child to attend to. She shooed Degna down the ladder in front of her and didn't think again about this missed opportunity until she received a telegram from Marconi.

～

April 15, 1912, dawned like so many other mornings, cool and crisp until the sun burned away the slight chill. The baby was over the worst of it, sleeping well, fever gone. Bea had checked in on him as soon as she rose from bed. She was now at breakfast on the patio, a place surrounded with wisteria and bougainvillea. She knew that Marconi had not made the voyage either, which gave her some comfort. Neither of them would be making celebratory history.

Marconi had written to Bea with pride about the new Marconi system they had installed on the *Titanic*. It included a Silent Room, a soundproofed room that housed the noisiest of the equipment: the transmitter and the motor generator, and a brand-new, 5-kilowatt spark gap transmitter. An ornate T-antenna ran the length of the ship. Marconi had been especially proud of his new invention, a rotary spark gap which gave the *Titanic* its own harmonic signature. When the *Titanic* called, everyone would know who it was.

The room was manned by two of his men, John George "Jack" Phillips and Harold Bride. Jack had been with the Marconi Company since 1906 and had just turned twenty-five days before the voyage. His nimble fingers could snap off a message in seconds. He had good ears, too, and could discern Morse code messages through a wash of sound that would seem like sonic pea soup to others.

Bride was twenty-two, almost Phillips's age but light years away in experience. This baby-faced operator had only been with Marconi for a year, but during that time, despite smoking three packs of cigarettes a day during constant breaks, he had proved to be a capable operator.

～

When Bea heard about the sinking of the *Titanic* and the fifteen hundred lost lives, she drew her children to her and wept. Degna could not understand why her mother was crying so hard, and Bea did not have the heart to tell her. She just hugged them and shivered while she breathed in the smell of her children. *They might have been on that ship.* Bea imagined the horror of it. She imagined herself losing sight of her children and hearing their screams. She felt the icy water, her final breath.

Her entire family had escaped an experience of sheer terror and almost certain death. She later heard that many relatives of the people who had gone down with the *Titanic* imagined their loved ones floating halfway between the ocean's choppy surface and the bottom—as the grieving relatives said, "Finding their own levels."

Marconi wrote to Bea that people were flooding his doors, asking about their relatives. As if he would know! He mourned the loss of the two wireless operators. He couldn't walk down the street without being recognized.

Marconi was now a superhero. Everywhere he went, people asked for his autograph. They grabbed his hand because he had saved someone, they grabbed his hand because he had failed to save someone. They sobbed, they smiled through tears.

Chapter Thirty

FIASCO WITH A FIAT: 1912

Ever since Marconi was a little boy, he had loved speed. It was the speed of the sailboats that had made his heart race. It was the exhilaration of the kite and the coursing wind he could feel through the vibrating string. Now, he had found automobiles. Whenever he could, he would drive and drive fast. He had a Rolls-Royce in New York, and in Italy he had purchased a burgundy 50-horsepower Fiat.

Marconi helped heft the picnic basket and luggage into the boot of the Fiat. It was 80 miles to Genoa, and he was looking forward to the curving roads along the Ligurian Sea. He had even bought a special silk scarf he hoped would flap dashingly in the wind.

Even though he had brought his driver, he wanted to be in control. So much of his life seemed out of his control. His family, his wife, the personnel intrigue at the Marconi Company, and the constant management of his various stations sometimes drove him to distraction. This drive would be a way to blow out the cobwebs of responsibility. For once, he could cut loose.

He instructed his secretary and his driver to take the back seat. He and Bea would be in the front. He glanced at her; she responded by looking down at her feet. Things had not been smooth between them. Marconi shrugged it off and started the car. It was brand-new and sprang to life immediately. It rumbled and trembled, and every bolt seemed to say, "Let me go!"

Marconi did.

They had just roared through Borghetto di Vara, a small town of flat stones and tile roofs. Old women looked up from their washing, and old men stared at them through rheumy eyes. They came to a notorious curve some people called Curva di Morte. Marconi took it too fast and had to spread out into the middle of the road. From around the blind corner came another automobile. Marconi saw it at the last second, but he couldn't avoid it. They crashed head on.

Marconi's last memory was a spinning, tilting landscape.

When he woke up, for a moment he couldn't understand where he was. He couldn't see anything, and all he could hear were murmuring voices, a squeaking wheel, and clanking sounds.

Someone was holding his hand. It was Bea.

She told him that one of his eyes had been speared by a splinter of glass. If they didn't take it out, it might affect the other eye. She told him, in a quiet voice, that he might be completely blind. As the doctor explained the details, she kept holding his hand. He gripped hers with his long fingers, and she winced.

Luckily, everyone else had escaped with only minor injuries.

Marconi endured the La Spezia military hospital for two months. An eye specialist eventually took out his damaged eye. For a while, Marconi was completely blind. Bea read the *Iliad* aloud to him, a book he had read as a child. Each night, she read until she was hoarse. They talked about next steps. If his blindness turned out to be permanent, Marconi could live at Villa Griffone and run his company from there.

Annie had come immediately. Although she was nearly seventy, her capacity for nursing her favorite son remained undiminished. She took the morning shifts and made sure that Guglielmo's bedsheets were changed every day, that fresh flowers were by his bed, that the nurses paid special attention. Marconi was not an easy patient, and it took women whose devotion exceeded his irascibility to nurse him. Most nurses avoided him and even chose straws over who would have to take care of the difficult Senor Marconi.

Everyone was surprised when, little by little, he began to regain sight in his remaining eye. He donned a piratical eyepatch, and by November, he was back to work.

Chapter Thirty-One

THE VOICE WAS IN HIS BLOOD: 1913

Sometimes, the ships Marconi traveled on felt like the narrow hallways at a high school. He was always bumping into people he knew. As he was taking his morning stroll down the decks of the *Olympic*, he rounded the corner to see Inez Milholland arm-in-arm with a broad-chested man in an orange and gray striped jacket. Inez excitedly introduced Marconi to Eugen Boissevain, her Dutch poet.

Eugen and Inez made a small, personal vortex of two. The focused interest they had in each other could have powered a bank. Marconi, a little jealous but very intrigued, had dinner with them that night. Eugen had a laugh that could be heard in the back row of any theater. He drank champagne and fed caviar to Inez on small orange crackers. They sat so close together that they could have held up a dime. Marconi sat back and enjoyed them as though he was at the cinema. They were a refreshing break from business and family.

He invited them to Eaglehurst and installed them in Luttrell's Tower. If any smugglers' ghosts were living in the tower, they were kept up for several nights. On the third morning, Eugen and Inez came into the main house hand-in-hand, looking like a tired Hansel and Gretel. They met Marconi in the estate's enormous kitchen. They poured themselves a pot of tea, seeming to Marconi like one creature, and asked if he would be best man at their wedding. He said he would be glad.

Things had been tense between Marconi and Bea. Although she had not given him any real reason, Marconi was constantly jealous, and he accused Beatrice of all sorts of infidelities. For her part, Bea was angry at being left alone, angry at having to raise their family on her own. She was lonely.

Eaglehurst was 80 miles from London and a million miles from London society. Although Bea loved her children, she sometimes tired of reading Beatrix Potter and only talking about dolls and toy trains. She yearned for adult conversation. When she mentioned this to Marconi, her comments often triggered an irrational response. He once threw a teacup at her, so close that she heard it whistle past her ear.

Marconi was in the garden with Degna, a precocious and intelligent five-year-old. He was trying to tie her hair back with ribbons, and she kept pulling away, playfully aware that he was becoming impatient. Whenever Marconi was with his children, he wondered why he was ever anywhere else. They were passionate, intelligent, wry, playful, and creative, the things he admired most in other people as well as in himself.

Bea came out with Giulio in her arms. She was aging well, he realized, as he watched her coming down the garden path. She had always carried herself regally. That was one of the attributes he had always admired about her, and as she tripped lightly down the walkway, he thought about how lucky he was. His family kept him grounded. The frequent letters he received from

Bea were filled with sound advice, and he realized he trusted her more than any other person on the planet.

Marconi had a new research obsession. He had always been possessed by ideas. They were his demons, his family. Morse code and conquering global distances had been his former passions, and now he was fascinated with wireless telephony: sending voice through the wireless. Instead of sparks, he thought about continuous oscillations. Instead of dots and dashes, he thought of human voices.

Perhaps his latest obsession began far back in those early days, when his mother would fill Villa Griffone with the sweetness of arias, cadenzas, and bel canto. She hummed when she was doing needlepoint, and she often broke out into a song as though it was a sonic sneeze she had no control over. She had taken him to operas, choral concerts, and simple folk concerts. The voice was in his blood.

His fantasy about sending voice included songs that could be heard by everyone, friends connecting over long distances, and family members staying in touch. Other people's dreams were not so lofty. They imagined seamen connecting with petty officers, petty officers connecting with ensigns, ensigns with lieutenants, lieutenants with captains, captains with admirals, and admirals with heads of state. Marconi's obsession would change the face of war.

War had been swirling around Marconi well before June 1914, when World War I began with the assassination of Archduke Ferdinand of Austria. Prior to that single bullet finding its target, Marconi stations had already been set up in multiple places of strife: Spain, Portugal, Egypt, Bangalore, Turkey, and Singapore, to name a few. Wireless technology had already changed the face of war, spreading light through its blinding fog.

The vortex of World War I would pull England into the muddy stew in August 1914. Italy declared neutrality. Marconi was in constant motion, careening like a pinball from America, to England, to Italy, to myriad other points on the globe, only occasionally seeing his family in London. His home base was now in Rome. He could sense the inevitability of Italy charging, even if half-heartedly, into the war.

Chapter Thirty-Two

WAR AND MARCONI: 1914

It is not clear whether the war reached out to Marconi, or Marconi reached out for the war. Perhaps they reached out for each other. In fairness, there was not a person, place, or thing in Europe that was untouched. Paranoia was rampant, and rumors of spies were everywhere in England. Three things combined to make some people wonder if Marconi was a spy: Italy's neutrality, the fact that Marconi was Italian, and his wireless setup at Eaglehurst.

Bea had gone shopping at her usual stores. Coming out of the bakery, she realized that clumps of people were "looking at her and whispering," as she later described it to Marconi. She immediately took Degna by the hand and made her way back to Eaglehurst. While Marconi was still free to gallivant around Europe, she didn't leave the estate again for two months.

As usual, Marconi couldn't stay still. He was in Rome enjoying new responsibilities, new medals, new honors. He received the title of senator of the realm from the King of Italy. He was now a bank president and a reserve lieutenant in the Italian Navy. He had joined the Italian Senate and received the Albert Medal from the Royal Society of Arts.

In a moment of relative quiet, he looked at his calendar and realized that for some reason, two entire days stretched out with nothing slated. He decided to take the opportunity to go for a drive and visit his childhood home, Villa Griffone.

Griffone had been languishing unlived in for several years. As Marconi pulled up in his Fiat (now driven at a relatively sedate pace), he marveled at how small it looked. The doorframes appeared to have shrunk, along with the roofline. He let himself in using the large brass key he always kept with him. The door shrieked, unused to opening, and the sound reverberated through the quiet of the house. The furniture was shrouded, the floor full of dust. Marconi sneezed. He ventured through the house, a time traveler.

There was the staircase where he had broken his arm when falling off the balustrade. There, the small dent where his father had accidently shoved a table too close to the wall. When he made his way upstairs, he entered his own room and stripped off the sheet. He lay down. His feet protruded over the end of the bed. He put his arms over his head, which he had always done when thinking. He was lying in a river of time. He saw his life starting in this place, gaining in speed as it rushed by him and into the future. He wondered how and where he would die.

That thought threw him out of bed and down the stairs. He began to look at his home with an engineer's eye. The roof needed patching, and there were windows that needed recaulking. The house could use regular airing. He made a mental note to hire someone from the village.

He stepped out of the house and into the backyard. He could almost hear the chuckling of the chickens and his mother's voice as she called to him from the kitchen door. He walked into the fields and could see his first kite, struggling to climb aloft. He left and drove home to Rome faster than normal, his one eye trying to do the work of two.

On his way back to Rome, he had a sudden impulse to visit his cousin, Daisy, now Daisy Prescott and a mother of three. She had done well for herself, marrying a banker, and Marconi was led into the back garden by a maid. He was sitting at a wrought iron table and had just been served tea when Daisy entered the scene.

She was heavier and slower, and time had wrinkled her, but she bounced toward him as always and gave him a peck on the cheek. Her voice was the same, a silvery cascade. As they had tea together, she described her life with her three boys, her husband, and her collection of butterflies, which numbered in the hundreds.

As they talked, Daisy looked at her cousin with a critical eye. He seemed haggard, his face a bit unshaven, his hair a bit uncombed. His false eye wandered around, disturbingly, on its own. He could feel her looking at him and he straightened up. He was brisk, brilliant, and when he rallied, he turned the charm on as though he switched on a light.

She remembered their sailing days, his attraction to the thrill, his thin chest as he lay on the deck under the sun. She wondered if she would ever see him again, for his sphere was enormous and encompassing, and she was a small thing, a little like the butterflies she had killed and pinned.

Chapter Thirty-Three

ITALY GOES TO WAR: 1915

When Marconi learned that Italy would join the war, he was in New York, meeting with his American board. The Italian government had requested that he return to Italy immediately to help set up wartime wireless communications.

On the day he was scheduled to leave, there was a knock on his door, and Inez burst in. She was going to quit her job, she announced excitedly, and become a wartime journalist. Marconi did everything he could to dissuade her. It was dangerous, he insisted. Rebellious. Foolish! Each word threw gasoline on her fiery desire. She had it all planned out: he was traveling on the SS *Saint Paul*, and she would accompany him. She knew he could open stubborn doors and silent mouths.

Inez could persuade Marconi of almost anything, and soon he was traveling incognito with her, steaming toward England on board the *St. Paul*.

German U-boats were known to be crisscrossing the Atlantic. Only months before, the RMS *Lusitania* had gone down with 1,200 lives lost. Marconi had been a frequent passenger on the luxury ocean liner, and when he heard the news, he thought about the purser who brought him his shoes and the bartender who knew his favorite wine. He had known them well.

As they arrived in London without mishap and walked down the gangplank, Marconi realized he had held his breath during the entire journey. He had been prepared to hide in the deepest part of the ship's hold if the enemy boarded. He knew he would be a spectacular technical catch.

Bea met them both at the station. She knew Inez, of course. Bea gave her a hug, and in that moment, Marconi suspected that at some point, they had talked. He found that idea vaguely unsettling. Inez returned her hug with vigor and swept Degna up in her arms in a familiar way. When Degna hugged Inez as well, he was even more bothered. As a rule, Degna was not one to hug women she didn't know.

He and Inez stayed for only a day in England. They loaded up an unimpressive black Fiat, a poor cousin to his own, and began the drive across war-torn Europe. Inez wrote in a small red notebook the entire way. She was not really a war correspondent; she was more of an anti-war correspondent. When they accidently ran over a rabbit, she used it as a metaphor for every life lost. Marconi, on the other hand, was not pro-war, but he was pro-Italy, and if Italy had declared war, so had he.

They argued for the whole trip. Inez kept trying to get him to see things her way—that war was irresponsible, expensive, immoral, and wrong. Meanwhile, he countered that war was sometimes necessary—a painful, horrible necessity.

They arrived in Rome hardly speaking. Inez, however, had her uses.

They were at the Hotel Girabaldi, dining on sole. Both had agreed to put the topic of war on hold, and they were talking about the Lipizzaners, the world-famous white stallions. Inez had just described seeing the splendid horses and watching them perform the "airs above the ground" dressage movements: the levade, the courbette, and the capriole.

They were about to trespass on their agreement—the conversation had trickled into a concern for the safety of the horses, who were almost all housed at the Lipica stud farm in Slovenia, which could easily become a victim of the war—when Inez squealed. She stood up, almost knocking the table over, and hugged a short man with a bald head, a pointy goatee, and pince-nez. Wearing a natty tan suit, he kissed Inez on the mouth and sat down at their table without asking permission.

Marconi was affronted until Inez introduced them. The man was Gabriele D'Annunzio, someone Marconi had often heard of but never met. A poet and playwright, he was almost as celebrated as Marconi, and it was a wonder their paths hadn't crossed before. Both were famous Italians and both were Italian nationalists.

As they began talking, they instantly knew they would become good friends. Feeling ignored, Inez occasionally rubbed her wine glass and made it sing so they would pay attention to her.

After five glasses of champagne, D'Annunzio stood up and recited "To an Impromptu of Chopin," one of his most popular poems:

When thou upon my breast art sleeping,
I hear across the midnight gray —
I hear the muffled note of weeping,
So near—so sad—so far away!

All night I hear the teardrops falling —
Each drop by drop—my heart must weep

I hear the falling blood-drops—lonely,
Whilst thou dost sleep—whilst thou dost sleep.

Inez noted that when D'Annunzio was in full oratory mode, his goatee waggled in an almost frantic way. Marconi applauded, and all pretense that war was a forbidden topic was dropped. The men began to talk about how Italians needed solidarity and protection. They were far-flung throughout a world full of anti-Italian sentiments. It wasn't right.

Inez did her best to add her voice, but it was as though the men were suddenly driving fast cars and she was walking. They talked until dawn. Inez stayed with them, but during the night her viewpoint changed. She had imagined D'Annunzio to be a man with heart and soul. Instead, she realized, he was a man filled with zealous nationalism. She forgave Marconi, but she couldn't forgive D'Annunzio, who had given poetry a black and military eye.

D'Annunzio, having worn down the political side of his brain, turned his eye toward Inez. As they walked out of the restaurant at dawn, he tried to seduce her, comparing her to a rare yet intelligent bird. She gave him an Italian gesture she had just learned and turned away.

As part of his duties to his homeland, Marconi set up wireless stations, met with generals and heads of state, and almost got blown to bits when he came too close to the front line. The life suited him. He enjoyed the adrenaline rush and the camaraderie of working men.

Among his other activities, he still managed to travel to England, where he donned his old hat of inventor. Working closely with Charles S. Franklin, one of his researchers, he started delving into shortwaves. The two discovered that if they used a certain parabolic reflector, they could focus the waves into a kind of beam, which was cheaper and more effective than unfocused waves.

One evening, Marconi attended a soiree at the home of one of his London-based friends. He was standing on the patio, admiring the night sky, when his attention was arrested by a beautiful aria that wafted out of the sitting room windows. It beckoned to him like the aroma of baking bread. He was a child again, listening to his mother singing in the garden.

Marconi went back inside to see the Irish opera singer Margaret Burke Sheridan singing Puccini's "Sola, perduta, abbandonata" with an Irish lilt. As soon as the last note had faded, he went down on knee, grasped her hand, and kissed it. Margaret, only twenty-six years old, looked down on him through blond lashes and smiled.

Marconi was entranced. Here was the antidote he had been looking for. She was his queen, his muse, his artist. He would own her. He would help her. He would make her a star.

Marconi took Margaret with him to Eaglehurst and introduced her to Bea. Bea was gracious and kind and fed the young singer sugar cookies fresh from the oven. Margaret was shy with Bea but came alive when playing with the children, for she had come from a large Irish family and knew how to make children squeal with laughter.

Marconi had decided to move his family to Rome, and he convinced Margaret to go with them. They all went together by train. The trip was a little like a circus, for Marconi was not used to traveling with children. Their noise was enough to drive him to the club car, where he enjoyed a fine Petite Sirah. Bea stayed with the children, Margaret, and their nannie. Bea did not take this opportunity to reconnect with Marconi. Instead, he got the feeling that she rather enjoyed the fact that the children with their noise drove him away from his new protégée.

They arrived in Rome and went straight to the Regina, a sumptuous hotel with tall domed ceilings and a gilt-covered lion outside. They steamed into their spacious new apartment, and the household transitioned into hotel living.

Margaret had her own suite at the end of a hall. It featured a canopy bed in one room and a grand piano in the other. Marconi got her the best opera teacher in Rome and made sure she practiced at least three hours a day. She was his songbird. He and his family often enjoyed personal concerts in the evenings, and afterwards, Degna would wriggle into Margaret's lap and play with the string of pearls that Marconi had given her.

Bea, sensing that the relationship between Marconi and Margaret was more along the lines of father-daughter, turned a blind eye to the expenditures and the attention. She had long ago realized that her husband's eye was not something she could retain, and she consoled herself with her own close circle of friends.

Besides, she was carrying Marconi's next child. She was six months pregnant, and this time, she was blessed with a dreamy attitude that had drifted down upon her like a gossamer shawl. She had realized that she was the mother—not only to her own children, but to Marconi himself. She was the person he wrote to when he was away. She was the person he needed to know was there for him, and generally, she was.

In April, Beatrice gave birth to a daughter they named Gioia. As usual, Marconi was away for the birth. Beatrice's body knew what to do, and as she remarked later to her sister, giving birth was easier than giving thanks. Because Gioia was born in Italy, he was a little Italian, and when Marconi returned, they celebrated by dressing him in green, white, and red.

Chapter Thirty-Four

THE END OF INEZ: 1916

A few months later, Marconi, by now wearing a uniform, was promoted to captain and was asked to begin installing wireless systems in dirigibles. He was out on an airfield near Rome when he received tragic news.

Inez had gone back to the United States to pursue the cause dearest to her heart: getting the vote for women. She was asked to participate in a major push that the leaders of the movement called the "Flying Envoy." They would travel to eleven states and give fifty speeches in thirty days. Inez could not resist the challenge.

On October 19, 1916, she was about to take the stage in Los Angeles. As she stood in the wings waiting for her cue, she realized that her heart was racing in her chest. She felt as though she could not possibly drag herself out under those blinding lights. The speaker before her finished, and the audience roared with approval. As Inez walked onto the stage, she felt as though she was walking into a desert. She fully expected to trip over a cactus. When she made it to the podium, she gripped the oak box tightly, as if it was a lifeboat, said "Ladies…," and collapsed.

When Inez awoke in the hospital, she knew she had very little time left. She had pushed herself for the cause, as the suffragists would say later. Her doctors had strongly advised against it, but as she said to a friend who sat near her bedside, she couldn't resist such a good party. As she grew close to death, she realized she could put even that to political use. Her last discernible words were, "Mr. President, how long must women wait for liberty?"

Unbeknownst to Marconi, Inez had not been healthy. She suffered from a number of ailments, including a serious one, aplastic anemia. The doctors had explained it to her. It had something to do with her blood. She laughed it off, saying it was just that her blood was not blue enough.

Marconi was devastated. When he visited her father in New York, he could not stop crying, and he commented that Inez was the woman he should have married.

It is difficult to understand Marconi's status at this time. He was one of the few people in the world who still traveled freely throughout Europe. The United States, England, and Italy all claimed him as a friend, and only occasionally were there whispers of espionage.

Marconi was now a diplomat for the Italian government. He was perfect for the job. He was an excellent speaker, knew the players in most of the important countries, and could travel from place to place with almost complete immunity. As the inventor of a world-changing invention, he constantly brought up its use as an instrument of peace, but he was also caught talking about it as an instrument of war. In truth, it was like most inventions and scientific discoveries. They are blasé until people use them, and it is how they are used that determines their moral status.

Marconi was now steeped in the activities of the war and feeling pressures from multiple sides. Everyone wanted this great man. Sometimes he felt like a glorified errand boy as he shuttled between Italy and England, acting as an emissary. There was no place of rest for him, least of all with his family. Contrary to all evidence, he was convinced that Bea was cheating on him.

It was past midnight when Marconi slipped through the door to his apartments in the Hotel Regina like a cat burglar. All was quiet. A single light burned low on a table—a night-light, for Degna often had nightmares. He tiptoed past the light and listened. He could hear breathing from the open doors. He slipped into Bea's bedroom and spied two lumps under the covers. He shrieked and turned on the light.

Bea sat up, jerked her sleeping mask from her face, and looked at him with wild eyes. He strode to the other side of the bed and quickly pulled the covers down, revealing…a long white pillow.

Without a word, Bea got out of bed and put her robe on. Her face was tight, and the skin around her mouth was white. She left the room without speaking to him.

He followed her to the sitting room, where she was holding a book in her lap. He saw that it was something new, Harley Granville-Barker's *The Secret Life*. "This is a play about frustrated relationships," was all she said. Marconi left for England the next day.

The war was exhausting, sucking the air out of everything. So many countries were now affected that it poisoned most wells, killed most sons, destabilized most ideas, and collapsed some governments. Russia was devastated, Germany driven back, and the Allies rallied to beat everyone else. Finally, in November 1918, the Allies and Germany agreed to an armistice. It was time to lay the weapons down.

Chapter Thirty-Five

It is hard to describe the impact of the end of war. Imagine pushing against a wall for years, and all at once, the wall disappears. Everything must be rethought. Marconi responded to this sudden shift by buying a luxury yacht.

Ever since sailing the *Sognare* with his cousin Daisy, Marconi had been happiest at sea. In his mind, he had finally created the best solution to his demanding work life: buy a yacht, trick it up as a laboratory, and sail to the places that needed him. In many ways, it was a brilliant idea.

The *Rovenska*, originally built in Scotland for the Archduchess Maria Theresa of Austria, purely for pleasure, was perfect. With its powerful coal-burning engine, it could go a brisk 10 knots, and now that German submarines were a thing of the past, they could glide safely from port to port. He would use its two tall masts for antenna, clear out the stateroom for his laboratory, and hit the high seas.

Marconi equipped his yacht with the latest in wireless technology. D'Annunzio called it the "snow-white miracle ship," and when he had time, he could often be seen on the stern deck sipping a mimosa. Marconi renamed it *Elettra*, an ancient word for amber, the fossilized resin that preserved specimens for science and produced sparks when rubbed together. It was the perfect name for a perfect yacht.

Submarines had grabbed his attention, and he wondered if he could invent a device capable of detecting them. He was interested in the idea of reflection. He had gotten the idea while staring down at the water that wrinkled and waved around the bow of the *Elettra*. He imagined a radio wave like an oscillating spear, heading toward the silvery water. What if waves could be reflected somehow and bounce back from the surface of the water? What if they could encounter something metal, such as a ship or a submarine, then bounce back and report to the sender exactly where that ship or submarine was? The key was shortwaves.

Reporters had gotten wind of such a device, and they hounded Marconi for information whenever they could. They would just have to wait. Marconi would talk about his new ideas when he was ready.

Now that the war was over, Marconi could engage in what he liked best: pure research. First, he needed to give up his role as diplomat. As he told British writer Harold Begbie in a long interview, he had drawn two conclusions: that diplomacy is not an exact science, and that it is easier to handle nature than human nature. He would go back to the business of business, and the business of science.

To explore his new ideas, Marconi needed partnerships with other companies. Partnerships were tricky, and each one required attention from monetary, political, and social points of view. Marconi excelled in all these areas. He made a deal with General Electric and salvaged his American Marconi Company, agreeing to transform it into something new, the Radio Corporation of America (RCA).

During this time of bargaining, cajoling, meeting, signing, and sweating, Marconi was on his yacht in the Mediterranean. One day, he was leaning over his workbench, a tuna salad untouched at his left, a half-full glass of chocolate on his right. The operator came up behind him and stood silent. Marconi was so wrapped up in what he was doing he did not even realize the man was there. Finally, reluctantly, the operator cleared his throat.

Marconi looked up with a distracted air. "News from London" was all the young man said. He handed him a message on paper and fled.

That was how Marconi learned that his mother, Annie, had died at Harley House, her London residence. She had been living there with his brother, Alfonso. She was eighty-one years old and had been ailing for some time. As Marconi read the message, the dots and dashes swam before his eyes. The operator had not bothered to translate it. Such small, innocuous patterns, delivering such devastating news.

Marconi took off his shoes, put on his pajamas, and went to bed. He stayed there for two weeks with a high fever. He missed Annie's funeral but heard later that it had been lovely, with Alfonso reading the eulogy and two of Bea's sisters spreading roses on the shiny white coffin.

Chapter Thirty-Six

"Welcome to our little kingdom!" D'Annunzio exclaimed, engulfing Marconi in a bear hug. The Fiume government building was not as large as most Marconi had stepped into, but it was filled with a lively group of stenographers, businessmen, priests, and militia. There was even a flower vendor, and Marconi bought a carnation for his buttonhole. He was hustled into a plush room, the sound deadened by a thick carpet and heavy drapes. D'Annunzio installed himself behind a large walnut desk, put his feet up on the desk, and offered Marconi a cigarette from a bronze box. Marconi declined.

Marconi had been asked to meet with D'Annunzio and dissuade him from his current course of action. In September 1919, D'Annunzio had led a military takeover of this small city, now officially part of the Kingdom of Serbs, Croats and Slovenes. A majority of the population was Italian, and D'Annunzio had come in with his nationalistic rhetoric, his chest-thumping, and his general stirring up of the populace. He was a poet, not a politician, and the powers that had leaned on Marconi wanted him to communicate this to his friend.

The conversation started well enough, for the two men had much in common. They both believed in the beauty and poetry of the Italian heart. They also believed that Italians were weakened by a lack of rigor and lacked imagination when it came to the modern world. They needed to grow strong, to gather together, to recognize the rights of Italians everywhere.

Marconi and D'Annunzio talked well into the night. Functionaries came and went, bringing platters of cheese and meats and pitchers of local beer.

D'Annunzio was at his finest. He was poetic, convincing, seductive. He told Marconi what he wanted to hear. Music was alive in this place. Poetry was the language of the country. The world that D'Annunzio had created by taking over this small corner was a paradise. Everyone was happy here. They all spoke Italian. They all respected the same flag.

D'Annunzio's eyes glowed when he told of his speeches to the masses. Marconi should have been there when he spoke from his balcony, D'Annunzio said. He should have felt the surge of Italian pride. It made the hairs on the back of your neck stand up!

He handed Marconi a postcard that featured D'Annunzio's dapper figure, dressed in a black shirt, jodhpurs, and boots. Beneath the photograph was the line *Hic Manebimus Optime* (Here we will stay, most excellently). D'Annunzio slapped his thigh and howled when he saw the reluctant smile on Marconi's face.

At that moment, Marconi's tragedy gelled.

He was there to persuade D'Annunzio to give up his grand plan. Instead, D'Annunzio convinced Marconi that his way was the right way—even though his way would lead to disaster. And soon, in 1923, Marconi became so convinced that the fascists would save Italy, he joined the National Fascist party.

D'Annunzio had tapped into an old frustration Marconi had against his home country. Early on, Marconi had offered his invention to the Italian government on a golden platter, and the government had turned him down flat. That slight, painful at such a tender age, was still an open sore, and he had never forgiven his homeland for being so shortsighted. It was as though Italy was Marconi's son—a boy who had potential but ultimately turned out to be a disappointment. It would take tough talk and tough love to make sure he turned out all right.

When Bea entered her new home for the first time, she thought she had died and gone to heaven. The air was perfumed with wild honeysuckle and lilies, the floor smelled of wax, and the singing of birds came through the open window. The vestibule she stood in included a long, curving staircase and a two-story ceiling. For the first time in her life, she owned a home. It made her heart sing.

The house was in Rome, just off the Villa Borghese gardens. From the second story window, Bea could gaze down on the tranquil lake and view the four-pillared monument on its edge. She could be at peace here. She could raise her children and be at peace.

Within two years, Marconi informed her that they needed to sell. When Marconi made that announcement, Bea had been bathing little Gioia. Her husband had walked into the house without warning, mounted the sweeping staircase, found her in the bath, told her he would be selling her home, and walked out.

She found him in the garden, smoking a cigarillo. Her feelings, caged up for years like a pride of lions, burst forth.

By the time she was finished, all of the statuary that had surrounded the garden was either broken or on its side. The next day, she moved to the Hotel de Russie, and Marconi moved to the Grand Hotel. They would never live under the same roof again.

Bea was done. She wanted a real life with a real partner. She would always care for Marconi, but she needed someone who would be there for her. For some time, there had been such a man, one Liborio Marignoli, Marchese di Montecorona. He had money and charm. Most importantly, he was interested in her as a woman, something she had needed for quite some time.

He was not a very attractive man. His face was somewhat squished, and his eyes were a tad too close to his nose. He had to wear thick glasses to see, and his beard was thin. But he adored her. They had met at one of the many parties in Rome, and he had played a mean game of whist. He had brought her canapes and goose pate. She wanted a divorce.

Strangely, Marconi did not jump at her offer. Bea had taken the place of his mother, a woman he could rely on for solid advice, the unvarnished truth, and a deep and unshakable love. These qualities were not commonly found. He had grown used to her as a helpmate and confidant. But Bea insisted. This time, she would have her way.

Marconi shuffled around for months. The divorce needed to be recognized in multiple countries. It needed to have every "i" dotted, every "t" crossed. D'Annunzio and his small country, Fiume, came to the rescue. In 1923, the Marconis filed divorce papers there, in the heart of the heartless.

Within three months, Bea married the Marchese di Montecorona. He was attentive, and she was in love. She and her children moved into the Marchese's rambling estate where the children could roam through gardens, chapels, and wine cellars, and swim in their choice of three ponds.

Chapter Thirty-Seven

Now that Marconi was officially divorced, the word took on a new meaning. He was unmoored, separated, disconnected, detached. He was unhappy. It was difficult for him to work. He felt old and ill and unwanted.

Then, in 1925, he met Cristina. Maria Cristina Bezzi-Scali was quiet, untraveled, serious, and shy. She had a soft way about her, a calmness that Marconi needed. She was aristocratic, and she was religious. This last point was a critical problem. Cristina was a part of a traditional Roman Catholic family, part of the so-called Black Nobility who had adhered to Catholic law for centuries. Although she was in love with Marconi and he with her, he was a divorced man, a condition that was untenable to the Catholics of her venerable family.

But Marconi was a man who had conquered space and time. The Catholic Church would not stand in the way of what he wanted. He applied the same systematic process to getting his marriage annulled that he applied to getting his inventions created, protected, and marketed. This problem, like any problem, could be solved. He just needed to understand the people, the politics, the rules.

He would go straight to the top.

~

Marconi's meeting with Pope Pius XI took place on November 4, 1926. Marconi was then fifty-two years old. The world was hurtling toward change. Earlier that month, Augusto Turati, the secretary of Italy's National Fascist Party, had made a speech in Rome saying that anyone who tried to assassinate Benito Mussolini would be executed. A French doctor had recently cautioned women not to dance the Charleston, since it could affect their ability to give birth. It was at this checkered moment in time that Marconi found himself in the same room with the pope.

He was led into a room in the Vatican that seemed made of red velvet. Pius XI sat at a table with carved cherubs for legs. His white robes emitted the faint smell of must. Marconi was uncharacteristically nervous. Here was the one man who could truly stand in the way of what he wanted and needed.

Marconi came armed with letters, documents, and affidavits. Everyone who had ever been associated with Bea or his marriage to her had been approached. Bea herself had been willing to say that when they had married, they had agreed that if it did not go well, they would part amicably and without ties.

They talked for five minutes. Marconi was just starting to warm up his skills of persuasion when the pope signaled with his index finger and Marconi was led out of the room. He still had all the papers in his hand, his heart was still pumping loudly in his chest, and yet he was walking down the hallway, an acolyte in front of him and one behind.

Three months later he received a notice from the church. He was free to marry.

~

On June 12, 1927, Cristina wore a white tulle veil and a long, lacy gown that flowed behind her in a train. She gripped Marconi's elbow as they stood at the altar of the Basilica in Rome. He was already her husband, for they had been married in a quiet civil ceremony three days earlier. She glanced at him out of the corner of her eye. He was fifty-three years old, she twenty-seven.

When she looked in the mirror that morning, she saw Marconi reflected in it—still in bed, his foot sticking out from beneath the bedsheets. She was married to a genius. A man who had changed the world. A man who had moved heaven, earth, and the Catholic church to marry her.

She frowned when she saw her own reflection and the wrinkles on her forehead. She hoped she could remain young for him. Young enough, anyway. She would support him, listen to him, and make his breakfast just the way he liked it: two hard-boiled eggs, two slices of bread, butter, and a cup of tea laced with chocolate. She would make sure his shoes and tie were tied, his hat free of lint, and his mind free of the countless small troubles of daily life.

In summer 1930, Marconi used his binoculars to spy the small boat that was speeding toward the *Elettra*. He could just make him out—broad-shouldered, wearing a blue boat blazer and a white nautical cap, a crisp white handkerchief peeking from his pocket. It was unmistakably Benito Mussolini. Marconi had finally talked Il Duce into meeting him on his yacht.

As Mussolini jaunted up the gangplank, he played to the camera. Giornale Luce, one of Mussolini's media projects, produced newsreels and was filming this momentous occasion.

Marconi and Mussolini were both at the top of their game. Mussolini was running Italy; Marconi was president of Consiglio Naazionale della Ricerche (CNR), Mussolini's government-led organization of science research. As they greeted each other, a pregnant Cristina stood to one side, a smiling, billowing white presence.

Marconi took Mussolini into the lab, had him don headsets and let him listen to the sounds of voices coming from miles away.

Over lunch, Mussolini swilled a big gulp of beer and wiped his mouth with the back of his hand. Marconi drank his Chablis. Cristina stirred two lumps of sugar into her tea. The sea was calm, the air brisk and salty, the sun mild. The seagulls squawked and prattled. Like them, Mussolini could not stop talking. His mouth was running away with ideas. He wanted to send his own voice out into the world.

When Marconi spoke about using radio to unite Italy, Mussolini finally stopped talking and listened. Marconi mentioned that the technology would take some effort, but Mussolini waved that thought away as though he was batting a fly. They would surmount any technical issues. They would do it for the glory of Italy. They would make Italy great again.

Marconi had always aligned himself with governments. He had first tried Italy and then gone on to benefit from relationships with England, the United States, Canada, and Ireland. Governments had the power to cross borders, to think big. In his mind, this was no different. Besides, there were real problems in Italy that Mussolini wanted to solve. Unemployment was rampant and people were striking in the streets. Under Mussolini's strict rule, Communism—which people feared like a political plague—would not have a chance. Il Duce was cracking the whip. Trains ran on time and telephone wires were being strung all over Rome. It was a new world, a technical world, and Marconi embraced it.

When Cristina gave birth to a little girl, it was the first time Marconi had been around for the birth of one of his children. He was like any other father and handed out cigars, his eyes glowing with pride. When he saw his wife, he took her hand and kissed it. When he saw his daughter, he named her on the spot: Maria Elettra, after his yacht.

Chapter Thirty-Eight

Marconi had met Lisa Sergio ten years ago at a party. He was in Florence, enjoying a glass of Chianti in the walnut-clad ballroom, listening to Debussy's new Violin Sonata in G minor at the Palazzo Wilson-Gattai. He saw a clump of men huddled around a small, energetic woman with dark hair and glasses. He was intrigued. She was talking seriously about politics and daintily toying with a large plate of *pasta al forno*.

Her father was Baron Agostino Sergio, and her mother was Margherita Fitzgerald, daughter of Charles Hoffman Fitzgerald of Baltimore. They had divorced when the baron had shot at Margherita with an eighteenth-century musket.

Like Marconi, Lisa was the product of two countries, two attitudes, two cultures. Born in Rome, she could speak fluent English and smoked Turkish tobacco. She was eloquent and erudite. Marconi thought her mind was like his Fiat. She could be overpowering, but she was fun.

For several months, they met each other in prearranged restaurants. They were never sure whether it would be politically problematic to be seen together, so they kept their meetings secret. For a time, Marconi couldn't get enough of her ability to analyze difficult political problems so neatly. It was as though she was cutting steak.

Within a few months, Lisa moved to Rome to start working for the *Italian Mail,* a weekly newspaper that covered Italian happenings and reported them to an English readership.

When Mussolini needed someone to translate his speeches so people could hear them in English, Marconi knew just who to turn to. He met Lisa on the Spanish Steps and told her he had recommended her for the job. He expected her to be grateful, but instead she sat on a step and smoked a cigarette. She didn't say anything until she had finished it, even though he kept asking her what she thought. Finally, she looked at him with a serious expression and said that she would do it—for a while.

Marconi was relieved. He had already told Mussolini that she would.

Women that Marconi knew kept popping up. He was aware that Margherita Sarfatti, a girl he had known in childhood who grew up to be a journalist and art critic, was writing about Novecento Italiano style, an art form associated with the Fascist party. He did not know that she had also become Mussolini's friend and confidant.

He found this out in the most peculiar way. He wanted to buy a painting. He happened to appreciate Novecento Italiano, for it was reminiscent of early Italian paintings: realistic and light-soaked, not like the tripe the modernists were indulging in.

He was visiting a gallery that was selling a particular painting. He had slipped through an open door and was about to call out to see if anyone was there when he became absorbed with the paintings. They seemed to speak to him directly, each with a different regional accent. There, the German milkmaid with her Jersey cow, speaking about the price of milk these days; there, the brocaded duchess with her small lapdog, chatting about the fox and hounds. There, the yawning, robust nude, slurring her words as she smiled at him, a rose in her hand.

He enjoyed this flight of fancy until he realized he was perceiving something else. He followed sounds to a green copper door in the back that was slightly ajar. When he pushed the door open, he saw two people he knew, Margherita Sarfatti and Mussolini, each trying to paint. It had become a competition, and each was as bad as the other.

When Mussolini saw Marconi, he lit a cigarette and waved a hand at his painting. Marconi mumbled something about "interesting technique." Mussolini was proud of his efforts. Margherita turned her painting over and shook his hand. She remembered him from all those years back and gave him a peck on the cheek. Marconi never bought the painting he had come for, but he left quickly, before he needed to tell any more lies to Mussolini.

After that, he saw Margherita often. She had written the book *Dux*, a biography of Mussolini that became a sensation, and she often advised Mussolini on what to say and when. In short, she was his propaganda advisor. Marconi was surprised when he read in the newspaper that she had been baptized. He had always thought her father was Jewish, and that at one point Margherita had been married to a Jew.

Chapter Thirty-Nine

THE ATTACK: 1935

Marconi had been pushing himself hard. Between his responsibilities with the CNR, which in truth he was neglecting, his obligations as a global spokesman, and his duties to his company, he had not rested in months. He also needed to put to rest a series of weird rumors. People were saying he had a "death ray" that could paralyze machines and burn flesh to a crisp. It could pass through steel walls and cause submarines to explode. Supposedly, there was nothing this "ray" could not do. It could turn people into machines. It could send them to parallel universes.

He was on the express train between Paris and Rome, sitting in the dining car, idly playing with a saltshaker and thinking about the power of rumors, when he felt a crushing weight on his chest. His heart pounded so loudly he could no longer hear the click-clacking of the train. The world began to spin and he fell to the floor, where he stared up at the striped ceiling.

Marconi heard a gentle voice talking to him in Italian. He felt someone push his sleeve up, followed by the sharp prick of a needle. He wondered if he was being saved or assassinated. A doctor happened to be in the dining car, and happened to have the right medicine to stabilize him. Marconi, who didn't often think about God, thought about him now.

Mussolini heard about Marconi's heart attack before the train had stopped. Multiple people met Marconi at the Roma Termini, the city's main train station. The doctor who had saved his life handed him over to Mussolini's personal physician, who bundled him into an unmarked hearse. "Nothing to worry about, move along," someone barked at the passersby. Marconi realized he was being cared for as though he was Adolph Hitler himself.

Marconi made a mental note to meet with Mussolini as soon as he was able. Rumors of his death were bad for business.

Marconi's head was buried in the morning paper. From his perspective, it was a morning like any other. Birds were singing, light streamed through the window, and he could hear the milkman as he delivered the milk. Cristina sat across from him, buttering his bread as usual. Then she began to talk. She spoke quietly, her words flowing from her as though they were a brook.

He tried to interrupt her several times, but she would not be stopped. Something was going on with the Jews. And with the Ethiopians. She had been at a luncheon yesterday, and there had been an incident. One of her good friends, Rachel Volterra, had been just about to sit down. She had brought the most beautiful roses and a small box of chocolates. She had set her gifts on the table when another woman stopped her, took her aside, and spoke to her earnestly in a low voice.

Cristina could see Rachel's face. At first, she appeared confused, her mouth forming a slight smile. Then she stopped smiling and backed away, her eyes wide. She turned and left the room.

The rest of the women took their places as though nothing had happened. The woman who had spoken to Rachel opened her box of chocolates and popped one into her mouth. Cristina did not know what to think until she inquired after the luncheon was over. Her friend Anna whispered that it was because Rachel was a Jew.

After Cristina finished speaking, Marconi said something that sounded like, "What do you know about Ethiopians?" and went back to reading his paper. Cristina shrunk inside. But then Marconi lay his paper down. He stood and walked to Cristina's side, put his slender fingers on her shoulder, and squeezed. "I've never understood that," he said. Then he returned to his chair. For a moment, their eyes met. Cristina could not read what was in her husband's eyes. She never mentioned it again.

Chapter Forty

Mussolini had asked Marconi to sit with the rest of his entourage on the balcony of the Hotel Albergo del Santo. Mussolini's birthday was nine days away, but he was celebrating early, since he would be on a yacht in the Mediterranean on the actual day. He had planned a demonstration of his robust nature and his ability to stir up raw emotion. His supporters were there to show their report for yet another bombastic speech.

Marconi had been in bed for the major part of two months. He was not in the pink, but more like a dull purple. He was, as he told Cristina, "diminished." Yet here he was in his black shirt, directly behind Mussolini as he spoke to the multitudes. Marconi noted the round microphones placed a foot away from Il Duce. He would be heard by the 50,000 people in the square, as well as by his new radio audience—thousands more. He noted that the back of Mussolini's neck bulged a little from his collar and was bright pink.

For a moment, Marconi tuned into what Mussolini was saying. "We do not argue with those who disagree with us, we destroy them. Let us have a dagger between our teeth, a bomb in our hands, and an infinite scorn in our hearts!" he shouted, raising his fists into the air. Marconi felt his heart thud in his chest and thought, Have I done the world good, or have I added a terrible menace? Have I truly helped the world, or just made it smaller?

He shielded his eyes from the glaring sun and was surprised to feel wetness on his cheeks. I'm overemotional because of my diminished state, he thought. I'm weak and ill, and sitting here in the blazing sun, trying to appear attentive…anyone would feel as I do.

He stared out over the rooftops and watched as flocks of gray pigeons wheeled across the sky. Ideas were like pigeons, soaring, changing direction, flying free in the air to be picked up by others, built on by others. In his mind, the pigeons transformed into sound waves. They flew in a vast circle, following the curve of the earth. He saw a future where the best opera singer could sing his current favorite aria, Puccini's *O mio babbino caro*, and it would be heard not only in the Teatro alla Scala in Milan but in the deepest jungle of Africa and on the tallest mountain in China.

The sound of 50,000 voices roaring their approval brought him back to reality. Mussolini, his barrel chest thrust out like a robin's, had clasped his hands in the air over his head. Marconi envisioned Il Duce's hair flattening under the wave of sound.

He wished Cristina was by his side. She softened any blows that came his way. She always stood in front of him when he felt ill or weakened. His mind wandered, visiting all the females he had known. There were so many. His mother; his cousin Daisy; Maria, the cook from his childhood who spoiled him with her lemon ricotta granita; even Bella, his first dog. Women glittered in his memory like lights on a Christmas tree; Josephine, Inez, Beatrice, Cristina…they had been the big ones. They were the dominant lights. What would the world be without women, he wondered? Certainly a less colorful place.

The balcony was filled with men. They sat in wooden chairs in their black shirts, their medals glinting in the sun, their heavy leather boots pointing straight out. Their expressions ranged from avidity to boredom, anger to scorn. He scanned the crowd in the square below. Mostly men. Their faces were turned up toward the balcony, toward Mussolini. Some had their fists in the air. Some had opened their mouths so wide they looked like little black caves. Thank God for women, Marconi thought. He almost stood up then, eager to get back to Cristina and their child, Elettra.

But he would have to wait. He would have to sit in the sun and listen to Benito as he incited the young men who would soon find themselves in another war. Everyone could feel it in the wind. Some spark would set things in motion, and the family dishes would come crashing down, just as they had when he was a boy.

He did not feel well. His heart was too big, the sounds around him too loud. The squealing feedback, Mussolini's booming voice, and the crowd's single voice pierced his temples.

Perhaps tomorrow he could think about this new idea, radar. Like so many good ideas, it had a certain elegance. Like a perfect aria, like a beautiful woman, like an antenna singing in the wind. So much to think about.

At that moment, he felt something give in his chest. It was as though a dam had burst. What do we think about when we know the end is near? They say our life flashes before our eyes. For Marconi, it settled like a butterfly on a single moment in 1895, when he heard a gunshot and danced in the dust. That was the moment that defined his life, when he knew he was destined for great things. He took a breath, trying to calm his furiously beating heart.

He saw a small boy in the crowd, in short pants, his hand raised in a salute. He had worn short pants once. He had played tug-of-war with Bella, and his mother had served him *Schiacciata alla Fiorentina*. He could smell vanilla, and the tang of oranges. His head drooped onto his chest. Time for a small nap, he thought, and at that moment, he heard Annie's voice saying, "Guglielmo, perhaps you and Bella should call this one a tie. You are wearing her out!"

Yes. Worn out. But I've done fine, he thought. I've given the world something new, and they will need to decide what to do with it. He closed his eyes and felt the air around him singing Francesco Maria Veracini's *Amor, dover, rispetto*, one of his mother's favorites.

Mussolini's bombastic rhetoric boomed through the crowds, aided by microphones and large speakers set up on either side of the balcony. He seemed to go on forever, but at last, he raised his fists in the air and finished, and the crowds roared, screamed, and gestured their approval. But Marconi heard none of it. When the speech was over and the men filed out of the balcony, he was discovered breathing shallowly in his chair. When they discovered him, he rallied and insisted that he walk down the stairs himself. He would not be seen lying in a stretcher, looking at his shoes. He took the stairs slowly, gripping the bannister as he went. He made it to an aide's Fiat Torino and collapsed tiredly in the backseat. There. He had made yet another long journey. They rushed him to the hospital where he would remain until the day that he died, a beautiful birdsong day, on July 20, 1937.

About the Author

Pamela Winfrey is an award-winning writer and curator.

As a writer, she specializes in writing surreal plays for a thinking audience. She is especially interested in the relationship between theater, reality, science, surrealism and mental health issues. She has received funding from the Sloan Foundation and the Marin Arts Council and was a finalist at Arts and Letters. She won an award at the Method and Madness Festival in Denton, Texas, and her work received the Audience Favorite and Best Actress awards at Variations Theater in Manhattan. Her plays have been seen as far away as Toronto and Ireland. She was one of the founding members of Mobius Operandi, an electro-acoustic sound sculpture ensemble and performance company which produced five large-scale, walk-through, site-specific performance pieces in San Francisco.

As a curator, Pamela represented the United States in the Interactive Art Panel at Ars Electronica (Linz), was the lead curatorial consultant for Emerging Artforms for Creative Capital, and curated more than 100 exhibitions, performances, artworks, and installations at the Exploratorium in San Francisco, where she is senior artist emeritus. She was the co-curator for the West Gallery, a gallery which explores human phenomena, and curated "The Changing Face of What is Normal," an exhibition on mental health that was dear to her heart. She has a B.A. in theater, an M.A. in interdisciplinary arts, and is currently getting her M.F.A. in screenwriting from Stephens College. www.pamelawinfrey.com

NOW AVAILABLE FROM THE MENTORIS PROJECT

America's Forgotten Founding Father
A Novel Based on the Life of Filippo Mazzei
by Rosanne Welch, PhD

A. P. Giannini—The People's Banker
by Francesca Valente

The Architect Who Changed Our World
A Novel Based on the Life of Andrea Palladio
by Pamela Winfrey

A Boxing Trainer's Journey
A Novel Based on the Life of Angelo Dundee
by Jonathan Brown

Breaking Barriers
A Novel Based on the Life of Laura Bassi
by Jule Selbo

Building Heaven's Ceiling
A Novel Based on the Life of Filippo Brunelleschi
by Joe Cline

Building Wealth
From Shoeshine Boy to Real Estate Magnate
by Robert Barbera

Building Wealth 101
How to Make Your Money Work for You
by Robert Barbera

Christopher Columbus: His Life and Discoveries
by Mario Di Giovanni

Dark Labyrinth
A Novel Based on the Life of Galileo Galilei
by Peter David Myers

Defying Danger
A Novel Based on the Life of Father Matteo Ricci
by Nicole Gregory

The Divine Proportions of Luca Pacioli
A Novel Based on the Life of Luca Pacioli
by W. A. W. Parker

Dreams of Discovery
A Novel Based on the Life of the Explorer John Cabot
by Jule Selbo

The Faithful
A Novel Based on the Life of Giuseppe Verdi
by Collin Mitchell

Fermi's Gifts
A Novel Based on the Life of Enrico Fermi
by Kate Fuglei

First Among Equals
A Novel Based on the Life of Cosimo de' Medici
by Francesco Massaccesi

God's Messenger
A Novel Based on the Life of Mother Frances X. Cabrini
by Nicole Gregory

Grace Notes
A Novel Based on the Life of Henry Mancini
by Stacia Raymond

Harvesting the American Dream
A Novel Based on the Life of Ernest Gallo
by Karen Richardson

Humble Servant of Truth
A Novel Based on the Life of Thomas Aquinas
by Margaret O'Reilly

Leonardo's Secret
A Novel Based on the Life of Leonardo da Vinci
by Peter David Myers

Little by Little We Won
A Novel Based on the Life of Angela Bambace
by Peg A. Lamphier, PhD

The Making of a Prince
A Novel Based on the Life of Niccolò Machiavelli
by Maurizio Marmorstein

A Man of Action Saving Liberty
A Novel Based on the Life of Giuseppe Garibaldi
by Rosanne Welch, PhD

No Person Above the Law
A Novel Based on the Life of Judge John J. Sirica
by Cynthia Cooper

Relentless Visionary: Alessandro Volta
by Michael Berick

Ride Into the Sun
A Novel Based on the Life of Scipio Africanus
by Patric Verrone

Soldier, Diplomat, Archaeologist
A Novel Based on the Bold Life of Louis Palma di Cesnola
by Peg A. Lamphier, PhD

The Soul of a Child
A Novel Based on the Life of Maria Montessori
by Kate Fuglei

What a Woman Can Do
A Novel Based on the Life of Artemisia Gentileschi
by Peg A. Lamphier, PhD

FUTURE TITLES FROM THE MENTORIS PROJECT

A Biography about Rita Levi-Montalcini
and
Novels Based on the Lives of:
Amerigo Vespucci
Andrea Doria
Antonin Scalia
Antonio Meucci
Buzzie Bavasi
Cesare Beccaria
Father Eusebio Francisco Kino
Federico Fellini
Frank Capra
Guido d'Arezzo
Harry Warren
Leonardo Fibonacci
Maria Gaetana Agnesi
Mario Andretti
Peter Rodino
Pietro Belluschi
Saint Augustine of Hippo
Saint Francis of Assisi
Vince Lombardi

For more information on these titles and
the Mentoris Project, please visit
www.mentorisproject.org

www.ingramcontent.com/pod-product-compliance
Lightning Source LLC
Chambersburg PA
CBHW060548190726
48283CB00003B/921